AS THE TIDES RETURN

Printed in the United States of America.

For more information, or to book an évent, contact :
rosetheauthor12@gmail.com
 @rose.k.wood on instagram
@ros3_asxtrism on tiktok
Rosekwoodbooks.com

Book design by Rose K. Wood
Cover design by Aethrastic Designs

ISBN - Paperback: 979-8-9914379-4-3
ISBN - Ebook: 979-8-9914379-3-6
ISBN – Hardback: 979-8-9914379-5-0

First Edition: June 26, 2025

10 9 8 7 6 5 4 3 2 1

AS THE TIDES RETURN

Rose K. Wood

Disclaimer

This series contains heavy topics such as cursing, character death, domestic abuse, gore, child death, genocide, torture, child abuse, child experimentation, knives and other sharp objects, racial discrimination, sexism, mass murder, and war.

Proceed at your own risk.

PLAYLIST

CHAEYA

RAVEN CLAN

SKYE

VEAPIS

DIRIAN

WYV

RAT'S   NORTHPASS
BURROW

ARCO   The forb

TROPITUS

ITA

XETHIA   KAGRIL

BOWE

ZIKA

N
W
E
S
Legend
Castle
Dragon Cave
Capitals
Vavia
Slosite
Busiya
Puthage
Dremore
Shezia
Fiore
Therith

PORT OF ARCO

RUINS OF BELLA MARIA

RED STRING
PATH

KELP FOREST

CASTLE OF ARCO

PARTICAL

E S

N W

SELIS

LEGEND

Ruins   Town

City   Ship

Castle   Kelp

    Cave

OF ARCO ◆ Cave of
Dragon Teoneinajoo

To all the oldest siblings in the world,
you are enough and you are loved
I see you
I know you <3

Chapter One

I was a king before I was even born. My father had planned my entire life out for me the moment he learned about my little fetus growing in my mother's womb. I don't think anyone would have been surprised if I ended up being born with a crown on my head.

To my father's disappointment and my mother's well-being, I was born as any other child was; naked and small. According to my father, I was blessed with all his genes and none of my mother's. I highly doubted it was a blessing. My mother was a beautiful and kind woman.

As soon as I could walk my father made me take many classes and training to teach me to be a proper prince. That was probably the only thing that ever mattered to him; that I was a proper prince, a perfect prince.

When I was four my life changed. One day my father came back from a vacation, nothing new. What was new was the baby his head maid was holding. A perfect little baby with pale skin, white hair, and bluish gills. My mother had immediately asked where this baby had come from. My father responded with a simple "doesn't matter, she's dead anyway." I knew even before anyone explained to me that this baby was my little brother.

Everett was everything good about the world. He was full of smiles and laughter, and energy. He was never very good at etiquette or studies, which labeled him a disappointment in my father's eyes. I never cared for that. Everett was good at other things, and he always tried his best.

Like any other kid, he awakened his magic at the age of four. Water magic, just like me and every Alion in history. He was born with offensive magic as well, but when he started his lessons, he preferred to use it defensively. I found it to be the cutest thing.

Arco was a kingdom under the waves, meaning that we were constantly surrounded by water, and many Arcoians preferred to stay in their animal forms or merpeople forms most of the time. It wasn't very uncommon to see guppies in half-animal form rather than their merpeople forms. Changing forms took a lot of control, and Everett took years to master it. I tried to help him as much as I could.

As I grew older, my father assigned me more and more tutors to prepare for the inevitable day I would take the throne. This meant that I barely had any time to spend with Everett. That's why after my archery training, I would immediately head to his room. We could talk about our days, and I would read him a lot of my favorite books. I think that was the main reason that he grew up to be a big bookworm. I do take responsibility for that.

Chapter Two

Everett finally got tutors of his own at the age of seven, which was just two years older than when I did. It showed me how much of a second thought my brother was to my father. As an illegitimate child, Everett would never have any claim to the throne, so he was utterly useless to my father. My mother was the one who had convinced him to let Everett have a tutor in the first place.

One afternoon, I strode into my mother's glorious parlor, exhausted from archery training all morning.

"Bourne." My mother called me over as I entered. I walked over to where she sat on a big couch, Everett, on the carpet below her, with a crayon and a piece of paper. His legs were replaced by his merfolk tail, and flapped around as he pursed his lips with concentration. His hair was long at the time and reached his chin in length. It was never the best hairstyle, but he was adamant about not cutting it. My mother sat on the couch with her tail out and a shawl over her shoulders. Her white hair braided in one long loose braid over her right shoulder, a gentle smile on her face.

"Mother." I greeted her, and she patted the spot next to her on the couch. I sat down and watched Everett for a second before gently kicking his tail. He jolted to attention and turned his head

back to look at me with an offended look on his face. I let out a small chuckle, and he pouted.

"Mother! Bourne is bullying me again!" He whined, and our mother just smiled and drew Everett into her arms. He nuzzled into her embrace and stopped whining instantly.

"Bourne, be nice." Mother scolded me with a small smile, and I smiled back.

"Alright, I'm sorry." I bent down to look directly at Everett's eyes. He pouted again.

"So, mean." He whispered, and I laughed. My mother patted Everett's hair to soothe him.

"Why don't you two go to the market?" She spoke up. Everett's pout turned to shock, and he looked up at her.

"Really?" He asked excitedly. Up until now, he had never been beyond the castle walls.

"You want me to be in charge of his first public appearance?" I sat upright in confusion.

"Your father can only keep him locked away for so long. As a prince of Arco, he should know his own kingdom." She nodded. I bit my cheek in slight panic.

"Does father know about this?" I asked. Everett struggled out of her arms and started swimming around the room in pure, unadulterated joy. "Do not worry about that. I will deal with him." She reassured me as the worry must have played clearly on my face.

"Mother, I-" she cut me off with a stern look.

"Bourne, my dear, please do what I ask of you." She pleaded. My mother was one of the few people whom I refused to disobey, so I nodded with my lips pressed in a thin line.

"Yes, mother." I stood and lifted Everett up onto my shoulders. He squealed and flapped his tail in joy. It thudded softly against my shoulder, but he was too light to actually hurt me in any way. I said goodbye to my mother as I walked out of the room. I took him to his room first so we could get into the appropriate attire for his first public appearance. Then we swam down the hallways to the castle gates.

Mother had prepared a carriage for us already, and the driver greeted us as we exited the castle doors. Since Everett was still a growing guppy, he was not strong enough to swim all the way into the city just yet. I also could not bear swimming at his slow speed, so a carriage was the best choice. In all honesty, carriages were rarely used for underwater travel in Arco.

I helped the excited little guppy onto the carriage. He refused to sit down and just swam in circles in the small space. I closed the carriage doors behind me, and we both looked out the windows as it began to move.

"What is the city like?" Everett asked me. I patted his head, messing up his hair, then setting it back into place.

"It is as I've told you before," I reassured him. "Nothing changes in just two days."

"Yes but tell me again!" He squealed, pulling on my shirt.

"Do not worry, you'll see it for yourself soon."

"How much longer?" He peered out at the vast ocean.

"Just a few more minutes." I patted his head. He watched as the rocky ocean terrain turned into a seaweed forest.

"When you get old enough to swim to the city, remember to follow the red string. It will keep you from getting lost in the seaweed." I informed him as we passed the red string path.

"Why is it red?" Everett asked me. I thought about the story my mother had told me years ago.

"Our dragon, Teoneinajoo, weaved it for her favorite Arcoian. But he had low vision, so she weaved in a bright red, so it stood out in the murkiness of the seaweed." I explained it.

"She has a favorite?" I nodded.

"All the dragons did. They are called the Chosen. The dragons loved their Chosen enough to give them some of their magic, and when the Chosen died, they passed their magic to their own Chosen. That's why our family has water magic."

"That's why? So, you're Chosen?"

"Yes, I am. You are, too." I pinched his nose. He yelped and stepped back, grabbing his nose. I laughed.

"I wonder who the other Chosen are." He looked out the window.

"You'll meet them soon enough. Many of them are royals like us."

"Really? I wonder if I could be friends with them." I patted his head.

"Anyone would want to be friends with you." I smile. He smiled back. I couldn't imagine why anyone wouldn't want to be friends with my adorable little brother.

Chapter Three

The carriage stopped in the city center. I got out first before Everett came jumping out.

"Don't go too far."' I warned him before he could swim off. A crowd was gathering around our carriage as the driver got out of his seat to spend time in the city. The royal family usually didn't leave the castle, so it must've been a spectacle for the people to see me and Everett.

"It's so big!" Everett squealed. I laughed as he swam circles around me, gasping at the big white stone buildings and the crowd of different Arcoians he had never seen. They watched us from a distance, but no one made any move to get closer to us. I bowed to my people to acknowledge their presence. Some bowed back, but others gasped as they saw Everett, who looked exactly like me and my father.

It was a widely known fact that my mother could not have another child, so I knew they were already making assumptions about this new child with royal blood. I moved slightly to hide Everett behind my tail just slightly. Many started whispering, and I instantly wanted to crowd my little brother back into the carriage and take him back to the safety of our castle.

"Hello! I'm Prince Everett of Arco!" Everett rounded me and shouted into the crowd. I groaned at his usual lack of situational context. I swam next to him and stood tall.

"Bow to your prince," I commanded, and the crowd bowed at their own pace.

"Why do they need to bow?" Everett asked.

"It's common courtesy to bow to the royal family. You're a prince, so they must bow when they see you." I explained.

"Oh. Every time?" He looked at the bowing crowd.

"Yes." I nodded as I took his hand. "What would you like to see first?"

"The market!" I nodded.

"This way." I led him through the crowd as they parted for us.

Selis was the capital of Arco and the closest to the castle of all the towns. All kinds of Arcoians walked the streets. Like every city in Wyvern, the city was built with white stones, the signature rock of the planet. The white gave a blue look under the water, so we just called it the blue city. To the south lay the many towns of the kingdom. To the east was the port that connected to the mainland. Somewhere between there and there were the ruins of Arco's greatest shipwreck, the Bella Maria.

Arco was a nation under the waves. We ruled every part of the ocean. At least we *did* until the breaking of the kingdom. We lost a small territory as the kingdom of Veapis, which claimed mostly colder waters and had even colder people, split from us. We were the biggest and second richest kingdom in all of Wyvern. Our dragon Teoneinajoo was also known as the kindest of all 10 dragons, according to legend.

Arcoians were some of the proudest people to live on this wonderful planet, and that fact was reflected in our clothing and the market. Pearls were everywhere; anyone you saw would be wearing pearls, the only jewel to grow underwater, worshipped by the lasting influence of Dragon Teoneinajoo's magic. They were also the symbol of the royal family, along with the wave and

8

the orca. The crest was printed on every piece of my clothing, a strong reminder to anyone I crossed paths with that I was a prince.

When Everett was three years old, I got him a white pearl bracelet for his birthday. My mother made him a pair of earrings made of pink pearls. He wore the bracelet at the time, but his earrings were tucked away into his dresser until he was old enough to get his ears pierced, which, according to Arcoian law, should be the age of 12 under parental supervision.

I held the hand with the bracelet as we walked into the market. He started pulling me over to a few shops. His excitement is incredibly evident in his body language. Usually, a prince shouldn't act like that, but Everett was always an exception to me. The only exception to my life.

"Look! Look at all the pearls!" He gasped as we entered a pearl shop. He swam around the shop looking at all the different pearls in their cases. Some were as big as my face, and others were small and imperfect.

"Do you like them?" I asked him.

"I do!" He squealed.

"Very well." I swam up to the turtle running the shop. "I'll buy everything he wants," I told him. The turtle looked at me, then Everett, before bowing.

"Thank you for your business, my prince." He said as he started taking notes using Arco's waterproof paper on whatever Everett spent more than two seconds looking at. I nodded in appreciation. Authority was one of my favorite parts of being a prince.

"Should I deliver it to the castle?" The turtle asked me.

"Yes. Bill the royal family for it."

We went into many stores looking at whatever caught my little brother's eye. Before I knew it, the streams of sunlight started decreasing, and the luminescent lights turned on one by one, painting the kingdom in neon greens and blues.

There was just one shop that was different from all the others. A black building, a signature of the Magic council. A man in the black robes of the Council and a water helmet stood just outside the store, showing a bunch of children something in his hands. Curious little Everett wanted to see, so he pushed his way through the crowd to the front. I followed him as the children parted for us. Eyes wide as they took in the blue of our hair and the glimmer of our white tails.

"Ah, a royal, the prince Bourne, I presume?" The councilman asked in the language of the council. I nodded my head. He looked down at Everett, and I could see his eyes narrow slightly through the helmet as he looked at my brother's white hair. "And this is?"

"My little brother Everett Alion," I explained.

"Interesting." He spoke. Everett was too busy looking at the small device in the man's hand.

"What is this?" Everett asked.

"This, little prince, is a device from my home planet. We call it a communicator. It allows us to talk over large distances." The councilman spoke to my brother in broken Arcoian.

"How?" Everett observed the brick-shaped device.

"It's quite complicated. I'm afraid I don't understand it myself." The councilman explained. He handed it to Everett. Everett turned it around a few times before he pried it open with his little fingers. The councilman let out a gasp as he tore the device from his hands. Everett let out a disappointed noise. I patted his back.

"I'm sorry, I'll pay for it," I told him. Everett began to cry, and I lifted him into my arms. "You can't do that," I whispered to my little brother.

"This wasn't for sale." The councilman narrowed his eyes at me and Everett in a distasteful way as he held the broken communicator in his hands close to his chest.

"I'll pay whatever price you want." The man's eyes narrowed on me, and I bit back anything my mind thought up about how foxlike he was.

"A thousand pearls." I stared at him in disbelief.

"What? I'll pay you in money." I explained.

"I don't want money." He stated.

"A thousand pearls are too much." Too much for someone with no royal blood. It was distasteful. Pearls were precious, and giving even one to another person was reserved for family or close friends and lovers only.

"This cost a lot on my home planet." I bit back my anger that was slowly rising. I might have made my lip bleed if I had bitten harder.

"This isn't your planet." I simply started.

"So, it should cost more." He had this awful grin. It wasn't about the device anymore. He was toying with me. He was enjoying playing with a prince. The fins on my arms flared with my anger.

"You are testing the royal family?"

"Are you willing to fight the council?" I felt anger rising in me as he called about the one thing I could not afford to fight. Everett continued sobbing on my shoulder as I comforted him.

"A thousand pearls. No more." I agreed, hating myself for giving in so easily. But the peace treaty between Wyvern and the council was a landmine of things I couldn't afford to set off. I knew that even as an eleven-year-old.

"Thank you for your generous gift, Your Highness." He said loud enough for everyone in the vicinity to hear. I couldn't say anything to him and risk ruining the reputation of the royal family. So, I just shut my mouth and swam away before I did anything stupid.

"I'm sorry." Everett pulled his head from my shoulder, having finally stopped crying. "I just wanted to see how it worked." He sniffed as he wiped his eyes. I smiled at him as he rubbed them red. I pulled his hands away so he wouldn't irritate them more.

"I know, but we can't break other people's things." He nodded in understanding. My little brother was always a smart kid.

"I won't do it again. I promise." He spoke as he hiccupped.

"Yeah, I know Everett. I'll buy you one so you can look at it, okay?"

"Really?" He asked with a huge smile.

11

"Yeah. I'll buy you anything you want to look at. Just ask me first, okay?" I patted his head.

"I will! Thank you, Bourne!" He hugged me and I smiled, holding him just a bit tighter.

"Oh wow..." He gasped over my shoulder. I turned to look at whatever had caught his eye this time.

Among the many shops in the market stood one bluer than the others. Many different blue paintings stood by the door. I swam closer. One was of the royal castle sitting on the cliff overlooking the city. That kind of view would be impossible because of the mountains that separated the kelp forest and the castle. Another was a painting of the white crested waves on the surface, the sun setting beautifully behind them, casting a beautiful orange glow. Everett reached out and touched a different one, which was a group of glowing jellyfish swimming in the depths of the ocean.

"Do you like this one?" I asked him. He nodded wordlessly as he traced his fingers over one of the bigger jellyfish. "Mother is a jellyfish," I said.

"Like these?" He asked and I nodded.

"You should see her."

"I want to." I laughed.

"I'll tell her that." Just then, the shop owner walked out and made eye contact with me.

"I'd like to buy this one," I told him.

"You have great taste, your highness. This is a piece done by the world-renowned Atlas. His paintings are a rare gem." He spoke as he removed the painting from its stand.

"Do you have more of his paintings?" I asked.

"I have one more yes. Would you like to see it?"

"Yes." He led us into the shop where I set Everett down so he could look at the many paintings. The shop owner led me deep into the shop where one painting stood covered by a cloth.

"Its name is *The Guppies View*." He spoke as if he had removed the cloth, and I felt my breath stop in my throat.

The shipwreck of Bella Maria sat among a coral reef; I could tell just from one look what ship it was. Sunlight beamed into the blue of the water around it, painting it almost green. The ship sat

12

beautiful and broken as fish swam through it and around it. Somewhere near the shipwreck was the shadow of a small guppy as they swam around the ship. The ship's figurehead, the famous Wave herself – the woman who united Arco after Dragon Teoneinajoo was killed in the dragon war stood proudly as if she were still leading the ship forward through a storm. The mast leaned slightly through the wreck, looking like it might fall on her at any moment and end her mission. In the middle of the painting was a single bubble, and if you looked close enough, you could see the reflection of a guppy's eye, confirming that this was from the view of a curious little guppy.

The painting was absolutely stunning, and I found myself at a loss for words. Everett had at one point come to stand next to me and gazed upon the painting with his wide purple eyes.

"I want that one." He spoke.

"I'll get it for you," I spoke after I found my voice once more. I turned to the shop owner, who smiled.

"Who is Atlas?" I asked him.

"They say he is a prodigy and the best painter of the century. His works are hard to come by, but no one has ever seen the man himself." The shop owner explained.

"If you get more of his work, I'll buy it."

"Thank you for your business." He bowed to me. He took the painting and started wrapping it nicely for us. Then he went out to the front to get the jellyfish painting. He packed it up and called up a younger man to help us carry it.

"Let's go home, Ev," I called my little brother, and he came swimming up to me. I held out my hand for him, and he held it. I bowed one last time to the shop owner before we left for the city center. Our carriage was parked exactly where we left it. The driver came running up and bowed before helping the young man put the paintings away in the back trunk. The seahorses bobbed their heads as we walked by them. I helped Everett onto the carriage and followed him in.

"Can we hang them in my room?" He asked in excitement.

"Yes. We'll decorate your walls with all sorts of paintings." I patted his head. He sat next to me, resting his head on my side. I hooked my arm around him and let him lean against me as the

13

carriage started moving. He fell asleep faster than I could blink. I smiled and patted his head again.

Chapter Four

I put Everett to sleep in his bed as soon as we got back to the castle. It wasn't hard after all that swimming and crying. I tucked him in and read him a fairytale before his eyes finally shut.

Everett's room was more spacious thanks to it being my old room. He had storybooks lying all over the floor and so many puzzles that would never be solved. I closed his curtains and put the paintings in a corner so he could decide where he wanted them tomorrow. Once I was at the door, I looked back at him.

"Good night," I whispered before I closed the door.

I was on my way to tell my mother about Everett's first time in the city when I heard the harsh voice of my father coming from my mother's parlor.

"Ariana! Who told you that you could let that brat out?"

"Please, Clyde, he's seven! At some point, he had to go out for his first public appearance." Came my mother's voice.

"He should never be introduced!" My footsteps slowed down as I got closer to the door.

"He is still your child!"

"I didn't ask him to be born to a fish!"

"Then you shouldn't have slept with one!" For the first time, I heard my mother's voice take on a fierce tone.

"Ariana..." My father's voice dropped in volume but still held a harder tone.

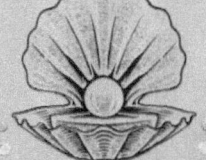

"No, Clyde, don't treat him like some disposable thing. Your mistake is the reason he is here, so take responsibility."

"I don't understand why you treat him like he's your child."

"Because, unlike you, I understand that he's a living being. That boy is your child, your blood, a prince." I peeked through the slight crack in the door. I could just make out my father's pacing figure and my mother standing in front of him.

"He's never going to be a true prince."

"Clyde!" My mother rushed up to him, but he struck her back. I rushed in to grab hold of her.

"Bourne!" My father called my name, and I looked up at his imposing figure. "You skipped your lessons this afternoon."

"I-I was taking Everett to town, father," I explained.

"Both of you are useless! Leave that brat alone and focus on more important things." He ran a hand through his hair in frustration. I helped my shaking mother to her feet and sat her down on her couch.

"Everett isn't a brat-" my father leaned close, his face right in front of me, and our eyes met. I could see the anger in them.

"Do not talk back to me, boy." I felt a dropping feeling in my stomach, and my voice stopped in my throat.

"Yes, father."

"Fix your mother. And never skip your lessons again." He said before he walked out of the room. I stood shaking, left in my thoughts, before the sobs of my mother brought me back to reality.

"Mother!" I rushed to her. She was hunched over, crying in her hands. Her hair was a mess. Her cheek was red from his hand/

"I'm so sorry, Bourne." She grabbed my hands. I knelt in front of her.

"He doesn't deserve any of this... if only he had been born to me..." Although I couldn't see her tears, I knew they were there. I felt tears pricking the edges of my own eyes.

"We're all he has, Bourne. That poor boy... why couldn't I be his mother?" She started blaming herself.

"It's not your fault, Mother. Lady Fate... Lady Fate is a cruel woman." I reassured her.

"Please, Bourne, my son, never stop treating him as he should be. Your brother." Her grip on my hands tightened, and she lifted her head to make eye contact with me. Her green eyes bore into my soul.

"I-I promise. He is my brother. I will never treat him as anything less." She pulled me in and hugged me. Her hand soothingly patted my head.

"My son. My dearest Bourne. Never be like your father."

"I swear I won't," I spoke into her shoulder as we held each other.

I found out the next morning that my father had packed my schedule with so many lessons that I couldn't find time to visit Everett. I checked the schedule for that week, and it was also fully packed. I realized what he had done. I stormed down to the archery range and just started firing one arrow after another. I wasn't even paying attention until my aide, Adrian, started clapping behind me and broke my focus.

"You're amazing, your highness!" He cheered. Adrian has been assigned to me since I was six years old. He was the same age as me, so it made sense to have him follow me around and build relationships in court by my side. His father was a nobleman who lived in one of the middle towns. He had red hair and grey eyes.

He was a giant squid, although not very giant yet, so his hair tended to change color when he got scared or was concentrating too hard. I thought it was the funniest thing. So, I didn't mind his presence, quite enjoying it actually. There were times when I wanted to punch him, of course.

"What?" I asked, confused about what he was clapping for.

"Your arrows all hit the red circle." He pointed down the range to the targets. Just as he said, every arrow I had shot landed somewhere within the smallest red circle. I stared at the strange sight, perplexed as if it had really been me that had done that. I

17

notched in another arrow, lifted my bow, and aimed. I drew the string back to my cheek, anchoring it there, and took a calm breath in. Then, on a random exhale, I let my anchor release and the arrow fly. The bow tilted down in my non-dominant hand as I held my posture through the next few seconds until the arrow hit its mark in the red circle. I let both my hands drop and stared in shock. Adrian started clapping again.

"Your aim just keeps getting better, your highness!" I looked down at my bow.

"I wasn't aware that I had gotten that good..." I muttered.

"You didn't? You have been getting better every day. Now you can shoot nearly perfectly!" He seemed like he had been the one to hit that shot instead of me.

"Congratulations, Your Highness." My archery tutor came up to me, clapping. "We can now start involving magic with your shots."

"Magic?" I asked.

"Yes, a normal bow and arrow are effective, but once you add magic, you can increase the number of things that you can do."

"Can you show me how?"

"Of course! Watch closely." My tutor grabbed his own bow and notched the arrow. Just as he prepared to fire the arrow, his eyes glowed as he activated his magic, and the arrow grew in size. He fired it, and it left a big hole in the target.

"Your magic shouldn't do that, but it's the same for the application. Draw." I got into the proper posture and drew my bow. "Now, before releasing, let your magic flow into the arrow." I tried to do as he did, but the water around me gathered and caused a whirlpool before imploding on itself and smacking all three of us back in different directions. I sat up and picked up the shattered pieces of my bow and arrow.

"We should get you a magic tutor..." My tutor sighed as he stood up. "I suppose elemental magic would be different in application..." He started mumbling to himself. Adrian rushed to my side and started picking me up.

"I'm fine," I told him and stood up on my own. "I've never had problems controlling my magic." I turned to my tutor. He nodded, and I thought he hadn't heard me.

"Yes. but this level of control would be difficult for anyone. Maybe I pushed you too far." I could feel the frustration of that idea bubbling up inside me. I had never struggled to grasp anything like this before.

"You can take it slow, your highness." Adrian tried to appease me. I ignored him and stormed inside the castle.

Over the next few days, I tried over and over again, to no avail, to implant my magic into my arrows, but each led to an implosion and a broken bow. After my sixth attempt, I kicked the pieces of the bow as far as I could in frustration.

"You really shouldn't be this mad," Adrian spoke as he watched my tantrum. "Not everything will be easy."

"I don't need you telling me that." I huffed as I kicked another piece.

"But you don't really seem to be trying."

"What?" I turned to glare at him. Immediately, his hair blended with the color of the wall.

"I-I just mean, you used to shoot at least thirty arrows a day, but recently you shot five and gave up... I know that the magic thing is hard, but maybe you could try just a little bit more?" He tried to shrink his presence. I walked up to him, about to tell him off, until I heard the voice of my little brother.

"Bourne!" I turned to look for where the voice was coming from and found Everett swimming full speed towards me. He contacted my chest and we both fell backwards, drifting a few feet as I held him.

"Everett?" He shouldn't have been anywhere near the training grounds or the archery range; he hadn't learned how to pick up any weapon yet.

"You didn't visit me for so long!" Everett picked his head up from my chest.

"What are you doing here?" I asked, confused but unable to be mad at him for too long.

"Visiting you!" He said as if it were the most obvious thing.

"This side of the castle grounds is dangerous, Ev," I warned him, and he pouted.

"But I missed you…" I smiled and hugged him.

"I missed you, too." After a moment, he wiggled out of my arms and started looking around.

"Whoa! So, this is the training grounds?" He asked, looking around at the open space like it was one of his storybooks.

"It is only *one* of the training grounds, your highness." Adrian stepped up, his hair drifting from the color of the walls back to red.

"There's more?" Everett gasped.

"Yes, this one is specifically for archery."

"Archery?" He took a while to pronounce that word.

"It's using a bow and arrow to hit a target." Adrian summed it up for them. "Your brother is a very skilled archer for being just eleven years old."

"Really? My big brother is the best!" I had originally opened my mouth to shoot down Adrian's unneeded praise, but the joy that boomed in my chest at my brother's praise made every word in my brain die for a second. I replicated the smile that seemed to be plastered forever on his face.

"Anyway! Are you done with practice?" Everett started pulling the sleeve of my shirt.

"Actually-" I started, before he immediately cut me off.

"We need to put up the paintings! You promised!" I don't remember *ever* promising him that, but his face told me he wasn't going to take no for an answer. Kids were the hardest people to argue with.

"You could have had a maid put it up for you." I patted his head.

"But I wanted to do it with you!"

"You can afford a little time off, Your Highness," Adrian spoke up. I looked at him and he smiled at me.

"YAY!" Everett screamed and started pulling me even more. I gave in and followed him. I could hear Adrian on my tail.

"What sort of paintings are we putting up?" Adrian asked. I didn't recall ever inviting him to help us, so the term 'we' threw me off. I turned to shoot him a glare.

"Some paintings we bought in the market a week ago," I stated.

"Really pretty paintings!" Everett jumped. Adrian smiled down at him.

"Do you like paintings, your highness?" Everett nodded his head vigorously.

"Yes! They're so pretty!" Adrian chuckled, and it made me mad for some reason.

"They don't have to be pretty." What was he? A philosopher?

"They don't?" Everett turned to look at Adrian while swimming backwards.

"No, they are about the feelings you feel when you look at them." I rolled my eyes.

"Walk faster." I turned to look at Adrian, who sped up.

"Sorry, your highness."

We entered Everett's room, where he rushed to the two, still covered, paintings resting in the corner. I removed the covers and let the paintings rest in the sun's stream for a few seconds. Adrian gasped, and when I turned to him, his hand was over his mouth.

"Beautiful, right?" Everett swam around me.

"Uh.. yes, your highness... very beautiful." He spoke in a daze. He was so weird and annoying.

"Where would you like to hang it?" I asked my little brother, patting his head as I picked up the painting. Everett took a long moment to look around his walls before pointing at one spot.

"There!" I swam up to that spot.

"Adrian, the nails," I called. After a few seconds, Adrian came swimming up with his red tail and placed the nail in the wall. He hammered away, and I hung the jellyfish painting over it. Everett was clapping in joy.

"What about the next one?"

"Next to it!" I nodded and moved over a bit. Adrian put in the next nail, and I hung it, adjusting it to make it straight. I nodded once I got it right. I swam down to Everett, who was clapping loudly.

"It looks good," I stated.

"I don't think princes are supposed to put up paintings on their own," Adrian said next to me.

"Well, if my brother wants my help, I can do it." I smiled at Everett, who was holding onto my shirt.

"You must love your brother a lot." Adrian smiled.

"Of course I do. He's my little brother." I picked Everett up into my arms.

"I want to learn how to make paintings too!" Everett exclaimed.

"I can see about getting you a tutor," I told him.

"I can teach him," Adrian spoke. I looked back at him. "I'm pretty well-versed in it..." I thought about it for a second. It *would* be better if he weren't following me everywhere all the time.

"Okay. But if Everett isn't happy with you, I will fire you." I warned him. He nodded his head furiously.

"I will do my best!"

"Alright." I put Everett on his bed. "I have to go to etiquette lessons now. Don't cause too much trouble." I patted his head and smiled.

"I won't!" He smiled back and waved as I left with Adrian on my toes. As I closed the doors behind I turned to Adrian.

"He has time in the mornings. Don't be late." I told him, and Adrian nodded his head.

Chapter Five

66 "Prince Bourne! Prince Bourne!" I was walking back to my room two years later, to change into more princely attire after a particularly hard morning at the archery range, when an elderly woman came swimming up to me. I had been practicing with a magic tutor, and against every bone in my body, it was helping. My aim just kept getting better, and I didn't cause little explosions anymore.

"Madame Volues." I greeted her as I removed my hair from its messy ponytail. I had spent the last two years growing it out, but it was now an awkward length. Everett had recently started hating his hair and had cut it short.

"I apologize for interrupting your day, but I just wanted to talk to you." Madame Volues was my math tutor until I got a new one at the age of ten. Now she taught my brother instead.

"Did Everett do something?" I asked. He recently started his mischievous phase.

"No, no, no! Quite the opposite actually." She smiled. She was a gentle woman, and that's why I gave her to Everett.

"Then what do you need to talk about?"

"The prince... he's a genius!" She exclaimed. I blinked in confusion.

"I'm sorry, what?"

"A genius! He picks up on formulas so fast, he learns at a rate far greater than any student I have ever taught. It is absolutely amazing!" She reached into the folder she was carrying. "Look at this." She handed me a piece of paper. "Advanced math that I haven't even taught *you* yet, but after just a few minutes of explaining it to him, he can answer most of the questions. Only a few are wrong, but those don't matter. Your highness, he is a genius!" Her eyes were so wide that she looked almost crazy. I looked at the math problems; some were hard even for me, but I could see the big red checks marking more than half the paper as correct.

"His cognitive abilities are unseen in anyone his age. It is simply the most amazing thing I have ever seen!" She kept rambling.

"My little brother... a genius," I spoke under my breath, and a big smile found its way onto my face. "Thank you for telling me, Madame Volues!" I handed her the paper back and swam as fast as I could to my brother's room. I slammed the door open to find Everett in the middle of the room, taking apart the newest council device I had bought for him. Adrian was off to the side, paintbrush in hand, and canvas in front of him. He turned his head to look at me as I entered, but Everett was focused on the inner workings of his newest toy. I ignored the fact that he was doing absolutely no teaching and rushed in and spun Everett around.

"My little brother, the genius!" I laughed. He yelped as I picked him straight off the floor and spun.

"Bourne! Put me down!"

"You are just amazing, Everett!" I smiled as I put him down.

"I haven't even done anything..." He fixed his shirt, which I had rumpled.

"Haven't done anything? You are solving teenage-level math at nine years old! That is something!"

"He is? That's amazing!" Adrian swam over to us. I ignored him.

"What do you want? A teleporter? Sweets? More paintings? Whatever you want, I'll buy it today." I smiled.

"I want to go to the shore." I paused.

"The shore? You can't even walk in water properly, yet."

"No, he's improving! We've been working on it!" Adrian cheered. That was not painting.

"Why are you here?" I asked him. "Your tutoring time is over." My eyes narrowed on him.

"I asked him to stay," Everett spoke. "Can we please, please, go to the shore!"

"If that's what you want." He started twirling. "But, only if you show me that you can transform properly."

"I can!" He turned his white tail into legs and stood on his bedroom floor. "See!" I nodded, clapping and smiling.

"Alright! We can go then. Put on some pants." I walked to his dresser to look for some pants. Once I found a good pair, I tossed it to him. He put him on clumsily, and I laughed. When he finally had his pants on, I held his hand as I led him to the carriage.

"I can swim now." He pouted.

"No, the shore is a day's swim. The carriage is faster." I told him as I helped him onto the carriage.

"One day I'm going to be such a fast swimmer that I don't need a carriage." He exclaimed. I smiled.

"I'll be waiting for that day."

The carriage stopped before the water got too shallow, since seahorses don't like to surface in their original form. So, I helped Everett out of the carriage, and we swam up to the shore together. He poked his head out of the water and groaned as the direct sunlight blinded him. I laughed and climbed onto the shore, swapping my tail for my legs. He stumbled out of the water and onto the sand.

"Wait, it's easier to walk here than underwater." His eyebrows furrowed. I nodded.

"We say you need to learn to walk underwater to make walking up here easier. It saves time." I shrugged.

"It's so bright out of here." He tried looking up at the sky but immediately dropped that idea.

"The water filters some of the light, so it's less bright. You'll get used to it after a while. A breeze blew by and nearly pushed him off his already shaky foundation.

"Is that wind?" He asked. I nodded as I stood up and dusted the sand off my hands.

Let's go look at the boats in the harbor." I motioned him to follow me. "Keep close, you'll get lost."

"Okay!" He followed me as I led him around the harbor, showing him the boats and ships. He looked up at them in awe.

"They're so big!" He gaped at them.

This is why we say swimming near the shore is dangerous. Your fins can get caught, and you could get caught.

"Okay... I'll be careful." I smiled and patted his head.

"Let's go to the lighthouse." I led him to the big lighthouse sitting on a large stone foundation. I loomed over the waves, a beacon for lost Arcoians to find their way home.

"It's so tall..." He gasped as he looked up to the top.

"Come on, let's go up."

"Up? Up there?" He asked.

"Yeah. It's very cool. You won't fall, I swear."

"Okay..." He followed me in, and we started climbing the stairs. We were halfway up when Everett stopped.

"My legs hurt!" He whined.

"We're almost there." I looked up at the top, which was just in view.

"Walking takes so much energy." I laughed.

"Swimming does, too, but you're just used to it. Practice makes perfect." I urged him. He pushed forward, whining with every step he took. I laughed as we finally made it up to the top and Everett fell to the floor dramatically.

"Come, look at the view, Ev." I walked to the balcony and looked outside at the lapping waves. Everett rushed forward before instantly moving backwards.

"What's wrong?" I watched him go back inside.

"It's scary..."

"There are railings, you won't fall." I held my hand out to him. He shook his head as tears started to fill his eyes.

"I don't want to." He stubbornly said. I sighed.

"Alright, we'll go down okay?" He nodded.

"You go first." He urged me. I laughed.

"Okay, if you fall, I'll cushion you." I started walking down with Everett close behind me. He held the end of my shirt as I walked. It was the cutest thing, and I hoped that my little brother would never grow up in my head. Ever since that day, he had feared heights.

A week later, I was called into the throne room for an audience with my father. I stood at the doors, taking deep breaths as I prepared to go in. I nodded to the guards to open the doors and walked in.

"Father." I stopped a few feet from the stairs to his throne and kneeled.

"Bourne. Good news, you're engaged." I felt like I was choking. I lifted my head.

"What?"

"Engaged." He repeated like it was something totally normal to tell your thirteen-year-old son.

"Father... I'm thirteen..." I spoke, and my father looked down at me from his throne with a cold stare.

"So? She's twelve. It's not like you're marrying her now." I felt my jaw drop, but pulled myself together.

"Yes... Thank you, Father..." I turned to leave.

"Bourne." My father called me. I turned back.

"Yes, father?"

"Don't ruin this. This engagement is very important to our kingdom." My father warned me, then waved me off. I exited the throne room and walked down the hallways of the castle. I looked out at the coral gardens as I walked. I could hear Adrian walking behind me. He hadn't entered the throne room, but he could clearly sense that I was not in the mood to talk. Still, he walked

behind me, three paces behind, following me back to my room
but not entering.

Chapter Six

I was doing a diplomatic mission in a town on the outskirts of the kingdom when I received the worst news of my life. It wasn't long after my fourteenth birthday. I rushed back as soon as I received the message from my little brother.

"Your highness!" Adrian's voice sounded from the hallways. I rushed towards it.

"How is she?" I asked him as soon as I found him. He couldn't look in my eyes and just stared at one of his tentacles instead.

"I'm afraid... she doesn't have long..." I felt my heart sinking and pushed past him into my mother's bedchambers.

"Mother!" I called, and under all the blankets, I spotted her frail hand reaching out, followed by the most heartbreaking sound.

"Bourne." She called me in a hoarse voice. I approached the bed where Everett lay on top of the blankets. His face was stained with tears as he rested his head where my mother's lap would be under the blankets. He had fallen asleep like that.

"What's happened? Mother?" I held her hand and spotted her face. She looked beyond tired, as if just staying awake was the hardest thing she could do.

"My sweet son..." Her hand reached up to touch my face. It was the softest touch I had ever felt in my life.

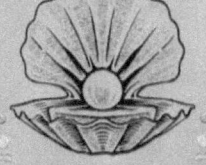

"Where is the doctor?" I asked.

"He tried his hardest, your highness... he really did." Adrian's voice sounded from behind me.

"So, he just left?! That's not trying!" I screamed at him, and Adrian sank back.

"Bourne..." my mother called again.

"I'm right here, mother. Right here." I clasped her hand, and she almost squeezed back.

"I love you." She spoke in a whisper.

"I love you too... I'm right here." I repeated, holding her hand to my mouth.

"Take care of your brother, please...." I nodded as I held back the tears. "He doesn't understand... not yet... so guide him."

"I will. I promise."

"And..." she gasped like speaking was hurting her. "Take care of yourself, too."

"Mother..."

"Make yourself happy too, Bourne... I won't always be here to take care of you." One of her jellyfish tentacles reached out and wrapped around my hand that was holding her.

"Please, mother..." I felt the tears falling, burning their way down their way down my face and floating off to mix with the ocean water.

"Stay strong... I don't know what will happen from now on, but... I'll always be with you...." Her voice started trailing off as her eyes forced themselves shut.

"Mother..." It was like she was rushing her words and her death.

"Both my darling sons..." She managed to smile one last time. Before I felt the strength in her hand leave. Her fingers started getting lighter until they started glowing and turned into small bubbles.

"Mother!" I held what I could of her closely, but just like all life under the sea, she was soon gone.

"May she return to the ocean of ancestors..." Adrian whispered behind me. "And return to the ocean which birthed her. Her soul, forever at peace for centuries to come. Everlasting peace. May her soul return and rest with her mother dragon." He finished the prayer. Then I felt a hand on my hand, rubbing small circles.

"I'm so sorry, Bourne." He whispered, wrapping his arms around me as I cried into my mother's sheets.

She died surrounded by her two sons, but her husband was nowhere to be seen in her last moments. I refused to believe he had ever loved her after that, and any love I might have had for him died with her.

Chapter Seven

It was like Queen Ariana Alion never even existed. No one talked about her. We had a small funeral, which felt very disrespectful for a queen. It felt like a part of my heart was lost, but everyone around me didn't even seem to mourn the passing of their queen. It made so much anger boil up inside of me. Everett had barely spoken since he woke up that day. I wasn't sure if he understood that mother would never come back but this little ten-year-old seemed to mourn more than an entire castle of grown men and women.

That made me angry. Everything made me angry.

Then there was Adrian. He gave me more space than usual. He didn't push me as much to get to the place on time anymore. He let me decide what place I wanted, and although it wasn't what my father wanted, he still did it. There were times when I would just burst into tears in the middle of doing something. Adrian would stand behind me, rubbing my back, and telling me it would be okay. It took me months to finally stop randomly crying. Everett soon returned to normal as well, but he felt the emptiness that mother had left for both of us.

Around a year after my mother's passing, I was informed that my fiancé would be coming to meet me with her parents. I was finally told things about her.

She was a Skyan, one of the many princesses of the royal family. She was training to be a night before the engagement, which princesses usually didn't do. I was told she was pretty, but I wouldn't be able to tell till I saw her.

The Skyan royal family was known for their many children. Five princesses and two princes. The oldest was an adult, married, and next in line to the throne. The second child was close to adulthood, but she was known to have an unusual illness. The third child was a boy who had left the family line years ago, so I couldn't really call him a prince. The fourth child, my fiancée, Princess Lin, was a strong, independent girl, just a year younger than me. Next were a pair of twins, not much was known about them other than one of them had ice magic. Finally, she was the youngest princess, a girl adopted into the family when she was young.

Skyans were people of the sky. They were children of the dragon Sukinaomo, the first dragon to die, way before the dragon war. Skye was the closest country to us, a kingdom of cliffy islands that stretch far into the sky. I had never been to it, but I did see the oldest daughter at royal parties before. If my fiancée were anything like her older sister, she would be beautiful.

Skyans were social creatures with a sense of freedom that was unmatched compared to any other people on Wyvern. I didn't understand how I could marry a girl who needed air and wind more than water. It would be very possible she would run away, not even a month into the marriage. Still, I was somewhat excited to meet the girl who would someday be my queen. If I could do anything better than my father, I could love her as she should be loved.

My father and I waited out at the castle gates for the Skyan king, queen, and my fiancée to arrive. They did not come that day. So, we decided to wait inside instead. When a week passed, and they were still not here, my father slammed his fist down on his throne.

"The disrespect!" He was seething with fury. I stood by his side as his heir as the border patrol reported no sightings of a Skyan carriage.

"Where is my general?" He called, his loud voice echoing off the throne room walls. I felt myself flinch.

"Here, sire." The general, who looked too old to still be in position, stepped forward.

"Prepare your troops and storm their borders."

"Sire, that would cause a war."

"So be it! They don't have the money or men to disrespect us like this."

"Yes, sire. I will have the troops attack." The general bowed and left the throne room. I wanted to tell my father off for his temper tantrum, but he was never in any mood to hear anyone speak down to him, and I valued my life far too much.

"A war with Skye will break any sort of partnerships and trading relations, Father."

"They started it. If they think they can look down on us simply because they have wings, they are wrong." He yelled. I bowed my head in submission. I was almost positive that the Skyans must've had a reasonable explanation for not showing up or sending even a letter.

When the troops attacked the Skyan borders, the Skyan refuted. Somehow, just as the old general had said, we were now in a full-out war with our neighboring kingdom.

Arcoians and Skyans had always been good friends; many Skyans ate the fish of our ocean, and we used their materials for hundreds of years. It started all the way back before the Dragon War. Our dragon, Teoneinajoo, and their dragon, Sukinaomo, were two of the closest siblings. Teoneinajoo loved her younger brother enough to pay him regular visits. The sky dragon was known for never leaving his cave unless he needed to; he never had visitors except his beloved older sister. With the two of them having such a good relationship naturally, Arcoians and Skyans maintained a close friendship as well. Now, almost 300 years later, we have declared war on our friends.

On top of that, the Magic Council did nothing to stop my father either. Everyone knew that Skye was one of the weakest

34

kingdoms of Wyvern due to the plague that hit them the hardest. With our resources, we would destroy them in no time. I felt bad for them, to my soul.

I knocked on the door, pulling my hood closer around my fins to hide my identity. The hallway was dimly lit with luminescent algae. When no one came to open the door, I knocked again, more urgently this time. Finally, the door opened and I shuffled in.

"What? Hey! Intrude-" Adrian started to shout, but I covered his mouth. His grey eyes were wide as he looked at me. I pulled the hood down and released him.

"Yo-your highness!" He gasped as I closed the door to his bedchambers.

"By the goddess, don't you know how to be quiet?!" I glared at him.

"I'm sorry. What are you doing here? At this time of night?" I looked around the room, confused. I walked to the center and looked around. His room was strangely filled with a bunch of paints and canvases, one covered by a cloth. It was far too small for my liking.

"I'm worried," I said as I walked over to the canvas.

"Wait!" He shouted, but I was already pulling the cloth down. I took in the red swirling with the blue to give birth to purple. A landscape of the sun setting over the waves of the ocean sat on the canvas. It was a finished painting that looked strangely familiar. My eyes trailed over every wave until the edge of the painting, where perfect cursive was written.

"By the goddess..." I gasped. I could hear Adrian sigh and turned to him. He was running a hand through his red hair, looking frustrated for the first time since I had met him.

"You just can't give anyone personal space, can you?" He groaned.

"You're Atlas?" I asked.

"Yes, and you're nosy." He brushed past me and took the white cloth from me, and put it back over the painting.

"Why didn't you tell me?" I turned as I watched him.

"Because I don't need to tell you everything." He turned back to face me and crossed his arms. "Now, why in the dragons are you here in the dead of night?"

"No, but why would you hide something like that?" I diverted the conversation back. He groaned.

"Why must you be the most stubborn person ever? I do not want to talk about this with you."

"I am your prince."

"Do I look like I care about that right now?" He looked at me dead in the eyes. I hardly recognized him. His red hair was messy with sleep, and his entire being seemed messy, unlike his usual put-together appearance. It made all my thoughts quiet.

"Fine."

"Yes, thank the goddess." He muttered.

"I am worried," I spoke.

"You said that already. What are you worried about?" He adjusted the cloth, then walked to his bed and sat. The audacity of his boy.

"This war. Something just doesn't seem right about any of this." I spoke.

"What?" He asked, looking confused.

"We have received no word from Skye, but they still fight us. They must have a reason. The engagement aside. Skye is a peaceful country. For 300 years, they haven't fought a single battle with any country, but suddenly they go all out? It just doesn't make sense." I explained all that seemed wrong with this entire ordeal.

"What are you implying?" He looked disinterested in what I was saying.

"A misunderstanding. I don't know what it is, but there has to be one." I grabbed his shoulders as I explained.

"Okay, what do you want to do about it?"

"I need to go to Skye and talk to the queen."

"No." He stated and I paused. He brushed my hands off his shoulders.

36

"What?" I blinked, confused.

"That is by far the stupidest idea I have ever heard. We are at war, and you are our prince. You think they will just let you walk into the kingdom without attacking you? You would be the biggest walking target to exist." He sighed and looked at me with a deadpan look.

"So, I just sit back and let this go on? We will destroy their kingdom." I groaned in frustration.

"Or you could die? Let their kingdom fall. You need to worry more about your own kingdom." He explained.

"Adrian!"

"This is exactly what I mean. You are the prince of Arco. One day, you will rule this kingdom, yet instead of caring about your own people, you focus more on your beloved brother or another country. You're just spoiled." I gasped at his rude comment.

"Excuse me?"

"I'm tired of this. You are a spoiled, stubborn, useless prince. Instead of telling any of these ideas to your father or just going about your plan, you come to me, a noble with even less power, as if you need permission. Then, when I say no, you get mad. If you really wanted to act, you would've been at the border by now. Don't you think there's something wrong here?" He walked closer to me as he spoke. I felt the urge to step back, but my pride held me in place.

"I don't need permission." I rebutted.

"Then why are you here?" He crossed his arms again.

"I-" He never let me finish.

"Go to sleep, your highness. I'll see you tomorrow morning." He shoved me out of his room and closed the door behind me. I stood in the dim hallways reeling from that conversation. Eventually, I made my way back to my room, unsure of what to do.

Chapter Eight

I never want to admit it, but Adrian was right. I was too much of a coward to actually go to Skye on my own. Instead, I paced the halls trying to come to terms with this new revelation. I was just walking down the same hallway for the third time when I saw a girl, standing alone, looking out at the coral gardens. She was small and had emerald, green hair and a water helmet on her head. I could see the small green bird's wings on her back and the flowy dress that she was wearing, which no Arcoian would wear. I approached her and cleared my throat.

"Are you lost?" I asked her in Skyan. She turned to me with wide, green eyes. I also noticed the little pink scar on the left side of her neck.

"Huh? Oh yes, I suppose so..." She muttered in a very polite tone.

"Where are you going?" I asked.

"The throne room. I'm seeking an audience with the king?" She said and I blinked.

"I can show you." I started swimming away, and she followed behind me. Her little legs could barely keep up with me, so I slowed down and shifted to my legs.

"Thank you so much...." She wanted to ask my name.

"Bourne."

"Zaria. Aquila." She said, and I instantly recognized her as part of the Skyan royal family. I nodded to acknowledge her.

"There's a war going on. Is it safe for you to be here?" I questioned and turned my head back to look at her over my shoulder. How had she done what I could not, but also look the same age as my little brother?

"Well, I just figured that if we just talked, things could end. I just wanted answers. I want to ask the king why they killed my parents. This war is not good. My sister is not in her right mind, no one in Skye is, and I believe it is my duty as the crown princess to save my kingdom..." She started running.

I paused at the mention of her parents. "I'm sorry, what did you say happened to your parents?" I asked.

"They were on their way to the engagement meeting. Somewhere on the way, they were attacked. Only my older sister, Lin, survived the attack. We don't know exactly what happened since she won't speak to anyone. She just sits in her bed looking out the window..." She fidgets with her fingers. My heart aches looking at her small form. She looks about the same age as Everett, meaning she was around ten, yet she somehow ended up trying to stop a war. It was a burden even I couldn't imagine.

"We didn't kill the queen and king. We thought they didn't show up because they were disrespecting us." I explained. Her head shot up to meet my eyes.

"Then why are we fighting?" She asked, a sorrowful look in her eyes.

"I don't know..." I muttered. Just then, I stopped at the two big doors to the throne room.

"Are you sure you want to do this?" I asked. If I were in her position, I couldn't even imagine what I would be feeling. My father wasn't an easy man to talk to either.

"I have, too. I am the kingdom's last defense..." She whispered, but I could see the hesitation in her eyes.

"Just breathe. I'll go in with you." Maybe it was her age that was so similar, but she reminded me of Everett, and that made something in my heart pulse. I smiled reassuringly at her. She tried to replicate my smile and nodded, taking a few deep breaths. I nodded to the guards stationed at the doors. They nodded back and opened the doors for us. I squared my shoulders and stood just slightly taller. Then I walked in with Zaria following me closely.

My father was talking to a bunch of his generals when we entered, and immediately his eyes zeroed in on me with annoyance.

"What is it?" He asked, his voice echoing off the walls.

"Father, you have a visitor." I bowed and moved to the side slightly to let him look at Zaria.

"By the dragons... You look exactly like your father." My father spoke. Zaria bowed in an elegant little curtsy.

"Greetings, your majesty." She spoke in Arcoian. I blinked at her pronunciation. It wasn't perfect, but it was impressive. "I am Zaria Aquila, crown princess of Skye."

"Crown princess? You? Don't you have three older sisters and an older brother?" My father asked as he waved the generals away.

"Yes... I was appointed by my sister, the queen." Zaria answered.

"Since when has your sister been queen?"

"Um, two months now, your majesty." She said, nervousness radiating off her.

"What happened to your mother and father?" He asked, leaning forward in his throne.

"Dead... for two months now." She spoke, her voice shaking slightly.

"What?" My father asked, confused.

"We were under the impression that you ordered them killed on their trip here..."

"Us? They never arrived at our borders." He huffed.

"Then... Can we talk about a treaty?" Her voice was getting quieter by the second.

"What?" My father seemed to be getting more and more annoyed by her timid display. Behind me, I heard the doors open and close, then Adrian stood next to me.

"I have been looking for you all morning." He whispered.

"Aren't you supposed to be with my brother?" I whispered back.

40

"That's what I was looking for you about." His words were rushed. I was about to yell at him before my father's voice shouted out.

"Speak louder!" I looked back at Zaria's shaking form.

"She wants a treaty," I spoke loudly and clearly. Everything in the room went silent as I stepped forward. Adrian's hand reached out to grab my arm.

"What are you doing?" He whispered.

"I don't know. I just acted..." I confessed.

"Treaty?" My father narrowed his eyes at me, and Adrian let go of my arm.

"Yes. They did not mean to wrong us, father. They are a kingdom in mourning. It is against Wyvern's laws to attack a mourning kingdom." I spoke. Zaria turned to look at me with a look of pure gratitude.

"Yes, it seems both our kingdoms just jumped to conclusions... let us put an end to this war, please." Zaria turned back and pleaded. It was clear that my father was already bored with the war and her presence.

"Is your sister still alive? The one who was engaged to my son." My father asked.

"She is... but she does not talk anymore... we do not know why..." She fidgeted with her dress.

"She's mute?" My father looked even more annoyed. "I don't need a mute daughter-in-law. We'll do a treaty, but the engagement is broken." He waved her off like she was just another annoying servant. The scribe came up to us.

"I will prepare a proper document and bring it to your sister." He told Zaria. Zaria bowed to him in a thank you. He looked surprised at that before urging her to stand properly. Zaria just smiled.

"You can leave. Bourne stays." Zaria was then escorted out of the throne room as I stayed behind with Adrian at my side. I heard his deep sigh and felt all the confidence I did have drained out of me. Stupid Adrian.

"That was stupid." He whispered to me, but I ignored him. For some reason, I felt empowered knowing that I had helped that little girl in some way. It was a nice feeling, and I wasn't going to let either Adrian or my father ruin it.

"You do not talk for others. Especially others that we are at war with." My father spoke, and I looked up at him on his throne.

"I know Father..." I spoke. "But she is only a child."

"That *child* is the crown princess by some wicked play of Lady Fate. She is not to be treated as just any child." He stressed. "You will take three more etiquette classes for your behavior today." He looked me dead in the eyes. Any confidence that I still had left disappeared at that moment.

"Yes, father..." I bowed. He dismissed me, and I walked out of the throne room with Adrian behind me.

"As I said, stupid." He spoke. I turned and glared at him. He shrugged. "Your brother is missing, by the way."

"What?!" I shouted.

"I couldn't find him anywhere on his side of the castle." He said.

"Why didn't you tell me sooner?!" I stressed.

"I tried to, but you were too busy." I didn't wait for him to finish before I shifted back into my tail and swam down the hallway.

I searched the entirety of Everett's side of the castle, but there was no sign of him anywhere. I checked my own side of the castle and still nothing. I was starting to get really worried when I heard chatting happening in the coral gardens. When I made my way over there, I could make out the two voices.

"This is not fair!" Everett's voice sounded, followed by laughter.

"How did you lose that easily?" I recognized it. Zaria Aquila. As I got closer, I could see the two of them huddling together, crouching to look at something on the ground.

"I don't understand this game," Everett whined. Zaria threw her head back in another laugh.

"I explained it five times already!"

"This is not fair," Everett repeated.

42

"Of course, not, but you're the one who asked me to play."

"You're supposed to go easy on me."

"I've never lost a game of marbles in my life." Zaria grinned.

"Everett," I called out to my little brother, and both of their heads lifted to look at me.

"Bourne!" Everett smiled and ran to me. Zaria stood up and fixed her crumpled dress.

"I've been looking everywhere for you. You have to take a maid when you decide to explore the castle." I scolded him, and he pouted.

"I was just walking in the gardens... then I met Zaria! She's my new best friend!" He pointed at Zaria, who was standing awkwardly by the cluster of marbles on the floor.

"Princess Zaria." I bowed my head to her, and she curtsied.

"Princess?" Everett asked with a confused look on his face.

"She's the crown princess of Skye," I told him.

"You didn't tell me you were a princess!" He gasped. Zaria fidgeted.

"Well... you didn't ask, so I thought you already knew..." She rubbed her arm.

"Wait, how old are you?" Everett ran up to her, comparing their heights, with Everett being just slightly taller than her.

"Ten." She spoke. Everett gasped.

"I'm older than you! I'm eleven! And my big brother is fifteen! He's so old." That last comment felt like a dagger to my heart when coming from him. Zaria nodded her head as she listened to him.

"My big brother is seventeen," Zaria added.

"Wow! He's even older." She nodded.

"My oldest sister is twenty-two, my second sister is twenty, my third sister is fourteen, my twin and I are ten, and my little sister is nine."

"You have so many sisters!" She nodded as he stated obvious facts. I wanted to commend her for her patience.

"Everett, she is a guest," I remembered my brother.

"But she's my best friend!" He pouted as he looked up at me.

"Everett," I warned.

"No, it's okay. I've never had friends outside of the castle." Zaria smiled softly.

"Me neither! We're going to be best friends forever!" Everett grabbed her hands, and both of them burst into wide grins. I inwardly groaned as I just had a feeling these two were going to be a huge hassle in the future.

Zaria looked past Everett at the darkening ocean around us and gasped.

"I promised my knights I would be back at the carriage by sunset!" She exclaimed.

"No! I held you here! I'm sorry!" Everett gasped.

"No, no. I wanted to help you, but I have to go now." She looked around.

"You're lost again, aren't you?" I asked with a small, amused smile. She gave me an apologetic smile.

"Let's talk her out, Ev." I patted my brother's back. He nodded his head profusely.

When we got to the front gates where two Skyan knights stood, it was just a little past sunset. One had maroon hair and the other had white hair. Both had red eyes and almost identical face shapes. They looked just a few years older than the princess herself. Their eyes lit up as they saw Zaria exit the castle.

"There you are!" The maroon-haired one shouted in Skyan as he approached her. I was shocked by how informal his tone was. "I was this close to storming in there and finding you."

"I'm sorry, I got lost." Zaria apologized.

"This is why we said we'd go with you!" The knight looked annoyed at her.

"Now now, Kousuke." The white haired one patted the other knights back. "We were worried sick about you, Zar." He had a softer tone and smiled at her.

"I'm fine. Not a scratch!" Zaria cheerfully raised her arms.

"Did it work?" Kousuke asked.

"Yep! The war will end soon!" Zaria smiled.

"You're absolutely amazing, Zar!" The white haired one clapped.

"And reckless," Kousuke muttered, crossing his arms.

"Kou!" The white haired elbowed him in the side.

"Ow. What? She's reckless, that's a fact." Kousuke grumbled.

"I'm sorry, I worried you two." Zaria's shoulders dropped.

"But Chika is right. Amazing." Kousuke added. Zaria's face lit up with a big smile.

"We should head back now. Moko's probably almost worried himself to death." Chika nodded towards the gates, where a carriage sat, in a bubble.

"You're leaving?" Everett gasped. Zaria turned to look at him with a sad look.

"I promised my brother I would be back in no more than two weeks." She nodded as she spoke.

"Promise me, I'll see you again?" Everett asked. Zaria smiled and held up her hand, extending just a pinky.

"Pinky promise." Everett smiled as he hooked his pinky with hers.

"Bye." Zaria waved as she climbed into her carriage.

"Bye!" Everett waved her off. I waved as well. She waved back.

Chapter Nine

We arrived in Skye just a month later to sign the treaty and attend the funeral of the king and queen. Two memorial stones sat next to each other, decorated with all kinds of flowers. More people than I have ever seen stood on the green cliff in quietness as a knight gave a memorial speech. In the crowd I spotted Zaria standing next to a blonde-haired teenager, her older brother. On her other side was another blond boy about the same height as her. I guessed that was her twin. Her older brother reached over and patted her shoulder, pulling her against his side as the new queen parted the crowd. Suri Aquila walked to the front and stood in front of her parent's memorials with a lack of emotion on her face. Her belly was slightly bulging, a sign of an obvious pregnancy. She recited the Skyan prayer before releasing a bunch of petals from her hand and the wind immediately swept them away and up. As soon as the last petal was out of view, gray clouds rolled in. Rain drizzled down on us as the crowd of on-lookers slowly dispersed.

With one last rub on her shoulder, Zaria's older brother stepped away to take some condolences from people. Everett let go of my hand and walked over to her. I followed him.

"Zaria." Everett called out to her, and she turned to look at us with a red eye.

"Everett!" She smiled at us with a small smile.

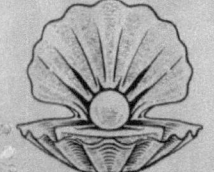

"I'm sorry for your loss," I said. She shook her head.

"Thank you." She nodded. Her brother beside her tapped her shoulder, and they shared a look.

"Oh! Everett, this is Mokoto, my twin. Mokoto, Everett. And this is Everett's big brother." She introduced herself. Her brother didn't look us in the eyes but nodded his head.

"Hello." He spoke softly.

"He's a little shy," Zaria explained. She was holding his hand, which was oddly covered in white gloves, and I could see him squeeze hers tightly.

"Hello!" Everett greeted him and he shrank behind his sister a little. I smiled at the stark contrast between the two siblings. Not only did they not look like twins, but they also had entirely different personalities.

"Oh, I'll show you around the castle." Zaria smiled.

"Thank you, Princess Zaria." I thanked her.

"That sounds weird. Just call me Zaria. You're older than me." She giggled. I pressed my lips together but still smiled.

The Skyan royal castle was built to confuse. The castle was newer than most castles of the 21 kingdoms, being built only about a decade ago. The design was done by Zaria's uncle, who was fascinated by magical artifacts. He built the castle, and when it was almost done, he enchanted it, giving it life. It was a very playful thing, purposely rearranging itself to trick its inhabitants. Yet, it seemed to have a soft spot for the twins, who effortlessly showed us each room.

If I hadn't met Zaria a month ago, I would've thought that Mokoto was a part of her from how he never seemed to leave her side.

"And this is our favorite room in the entire castle!" Zaria pushed the Everwood doors open, and Mokoto walked in first. As we entered, a Skyan breeze nearly blew me off my feet. I heard pages fluttering and beautiful rays of sun streaked in from the open windows. It was breezy, but it felt amazingly warm. In front of us were rows upon rows of bookshelves. A few tables sat all around the room, but I couldn't even see the other side because of how large the entire room was. The weird thing was that from the outside, the castle didn't even look that large, but each room was large and luxurious. As we strolled through the rows of books, I couldn't see a speck of dust on any of the books or shelves. It was clear that this entire castle was always kept in its best condition. The entire room was filled with the scent of Everwood, which smelled a lot like pine but darker, and books. Many looked decades old. It was such a peaceful environment.

Everett kept staring at the books with his mouth wide open. I held in a laugh that bubbled up into my throat.

"There are so many books!" He finally muttered with a bewildered expression. "Where did they all come from?"

"People wrote them. Our family has been collecting them for years. It was my grandfather's pride, so my uncle put as much work into the library as possible. Then it became my mother's, and she shared it with us."

"Have you read all of them?" He asked her.

"Oh no, I'm not allowed to read the adult books just yet. But I've read all the books on this side of the library." She pointed to our right, which held at least five rows of shelves. I tried to reason with myself whether she was lying or not.

"How do you find the time for that?" I asked. I could tell from her manners that she definitely attended etiquette classes. How she had time outside of classes was impressive.

"I'm not allowed into town yet, so I have a bunch of time." She shrugs as we walk deeper into the library.

"What's that?" Everett points to an open hatch that descends below the library.

"Oh, that? Wanna see?" She turned to us with a mischievous little grin on her face. I had a bad feeling.

"Are we allowed down there?" I asked her.

"I'm not sure. Mokoto and I are the only people who know about it." Mokoto walked up to the hatch and pulled it open just a bit more. We gathered around it and looked down. I could make out the outline of the stairs, but it was way too dark to be safe.

"How many times have you been down there?" I was concerned about how these two haven't broken a bone yet.

48

"It's not like we count." Zaria rolled her eyes. "Castle." She called, and the dark passageway lit up with torches in a wave. Mokoto went first, and Zaria followed. Everett was already bouncing down the stairs before I could say anything. I followed to make sure neither of these three got hurt, not because I was curious.

We walked down the stairs for a while before the narrow passage widened into a whole other library. Seriously, where did they even get this many books? This one didn't have rows of bookshelves. Instead, the walls were the shelves themselves. The room was shaped in an odd, flower-like shape, with each shelf towering high over us and filled to the brim with books and scrolls. I walked up to the closest wall and plucked a book off the shelf. The cover was just a plain green, with rips and tears everywhere, a sign of its age. No title in sight. I opened it to the title page, but none of the words made sense. It was written in a language I had yet to learn. I placed the book back and picked another to find only the same thing.

"Are all of these foreign?" I asked as I opened one book after another.

"Yep! There are some here that are in dead languages as well." Zaria walked around with a little pep in her step, like this was her natural environment.

Unlike the library upstairs, this one was darker, more meaningful in a way I couldn't quite understand. The windows weren't open but instead filled with colored glass artwork, painting the room in rainbows as the light streamed in. There was nowhere for the eternal winds outside to get in, yet there was just the smallest little breeze, the most pleasing breeze I had ever felt.

"Dead languages?" I asked when I grabbed another book, this one's cover engraved with a flower that I couldn't identify even if I liked flowers.

"Dragon tongue, old Skyan, trades tongue, fire tongue." She listed on her fingers. "All languages that haven't been heard or taught in centuries."

49

"You can tell them apart?" I was confused as to how she knew what specific languages these books were likely written in. She shrugged.

"You can usually tell when and where the book was written based on the color of the pages, binding of the book, style, and handwriting. Then you just make a guess of where the book most likely came from, and you can guess the language." She said it like it was the easiest thing to understand. It reminded me of how Everett would explain his math homework to me or the devices he tinkered with.

"Zaria loves history." Mokoto spoke in a quiet voice that in this closed space echoed slightly off the walls. It surprised me slightly as he hadn't said anything to us since he had said hello earlier that day. "It's... weird." He shrugged and scrunched his face like that word personally offended him, but he couldn't find a better term.

"It's not weird! It's a hobby!" Zaria shrieked and pouted. Mokoto nodded like he was siding with her, but his face said otherwise, a look of boredom plastered on it.

"I don't think it's weird!" Everett smiled. "I like math and art! What about you?" He took a step closer to the golden-haired prince, who in return leaned back like proximity to anyone but his sister was life-threatening.

"I like stars... and maps..." Mokoto muttered. He strolled over to a different wall, this one filled with scrolls instead of books, and pulled one scroll out. It was rolled and tied with a dark blue ribbon, which he undid. He rolled the scroll out and held it open for us to see. A beautifully illustrated map of Skye sat on the scroll, painstakingly detailed. I could only imagine how long creating it must have taken.

"One day..." he started, his voice slowly getting just a bit louder like he was finally getting comfortable with us. "I'm going to map the sky." He spoke.

"The sky?" I asked.

"You mean the stars?" Everett guessed, and he nodded.

"There are so many of them, though..." I muttered, questioning if it was even possible.

"I know…" Mokoto's face turned into a slight pout, and I could finally see how he was Zaria's twin. Although they had different hair and eyes, their facial structures were identical, like someone copied one twin's face and pasted it onto the other. The only difference was the small little mole just below Zaria's right eye and the pink scar on her neck. Mokoto's mole was just below his lip on the left side of his face.

"He can do it!" Zaria patted her brother's shoulder with a big smile on her face. "I just know he can!" Mokoto's face replicated the smile in a display of the most emotion I had seen on his face yet.

Later that day I was walking in the cloud garden, an entire garden filled with flowers and cloud sculptures. I had no idea how one would make a sculpture out of clouds, but they did. There were so many of them as well. The tallest was the sculpture of the Sun King, an old Skyan king who did something to save the kingdom in a time of need. I never cared about history like that, but I did sit through an entire history lesson by Zaria and not remember a single thing. That girl was crazy, and that was a compliment, I think. How she remembered so many facts about just the randomest things was beyond me.

I heard rustling from some bushes and went to investigate, not my best moment.

A sword tip stopped just short of my nose. Bright golden eyes at the other end burned into me as I took a forced step back.

"Am I trespassing?" I held up my hands to show her I was of no threat. The girl with golden hair, a close copy of Mokoto, but taller, dragged her eyes over me. Then she lowered her sword and sheathed it. I ran through the options on which Aquila this was. Queen Suri was older than her; Akemi would be in a wheelchair, and Mokoto was a boy. That would leave only one Aquila, the one that was betrothed to me just two months ago. Lin Aquila. I was right, she was just as pretty as her older sister, maybe even prettier. She wore a white tunic that was dirtied from the dirt around her. Her golden hair is dirtier blond and falling

51

over her shoulder in a sloppy ponytail. On her legs were brown training pants, and I could see the calluses on her hands from swinging her sword. Her wings were folded neatly behind her, brown and unruffled. She bowed to me as she recognized me. I bowed back in respect. She turned to leave, and I called out to her.

"Um, hello, Princess Lin, right?" She stopped and turned back to me. Our eyes met and I really wanted to just know what she was thinking about. She nodded her head.

"I'm Prince Bourne... I was betrothed to you..." I realized that my words might remind her of her parents' murder, and inwardly punched myself. She looked down at the ground and then nodded.

"Um... can I just ask if you're alright?" I took a nervous step forward. She looked back up at me, the setting sun reflecting beautifully in her golden eyes. Her stoic face turned into one of the sweetest smiles I had ever seen. She nodded her head again and then turned and left. I blinked as my mind tried to process just how weird every member of this family was when it came to manners.

After that day, visiting the twins became almost normal to us. We would go every few months. To our father, it was a way to build positive relations with Skye again after the war, but to us, it was friends meeting up.

I later found out that Zaria had telekinesis magic and Mokoto had ice magic. It came as a surprise to find out that a Skyan had been given ice elemental magic, but the Chosen weren't always exclusively native to the land their powers belonged to. It was just slightly unheard of.

Of the original 10 dragons, only nine had created their own lands surrounding the main dragon lands, which we now call the forbidden lands. The name was given in respect to the only surviving dragon of Wyvern. In her own cave, she slept until she decided to leave, as each dragon did. They passed on their powers to the person they trusted the most. This is how the elemental magics were born, so it made sense for the Chosen to be from the land to which their power originated from. Only two dragons never passed on their power.

That was the dragon of the sky who died way before the Dragon war, and the dragon of fire, whose entire civilization disappeared with her during the Dragon war. So currently, in Wyvern, only seven elements exist. The last dragon, Arli, never shared her powers.

Our family was one of the descendants of a Chosen, so it makes sense that we inherited water magic through most of our bloodline. Other countries follow the same kind of rule, but some don't. The land of lightning, having been overthrown in war. As to why the previous user of ice had chosen this random Skyan boy over someone originating from the land of ice was probably the biggest mystery of our modern day. Of course, Chosen didn't have to be dead before they could pass on the powers, but the person that they gave their powers to has to have not been born yet for magic to exist in a person the moment they are born.

There was just one group of people on Wyvern that seemed not to follow these rules, and of course, you wouldn't be surprised to hear that they weren't even from Wyvern. The Magic Council came from a planet far from ours with different systems of living. They were people without magic, and when they first arrived in Wyvern, no one trusted them, and they never trusted us. Somehow, against all odds, they managed to become the only thing keeping the entirety of Wyvern from being the peaceful planet that it was originally made to be. In all honesty, we knew nothing about the council and the planet that came from. All we knew was that the Goddess had given them birth, and they somehow had destroyed her trust enough for them to feel they had to flee their own planet. Yet they only arrived with mainly men. No one could exactly figure out where all the women were. It's not like the men could just randomly reproduce themselves. That was proven false long ago, but no one really knew exactly what was happening with the council. No one had cracked the puzzle. The Magic Council ruled over all of Wyvern, even though they had no ties to this planet and no reason to want to rule it. They could not harvest the power that grew in our lands. They could not use the magic that flow freely through the world and they could not understand half the things that we were accustomed with from birth, but they sure acted like they did and I am not one to speak against something as powerful as the Council, but I did believe that one day they would push just a little too hard.

Chapter Ten

Queen Suri, Zaria's oldest sister, went into labor not long after the funeral. It was also around that time that Zaria started sending us letters. She told us about her new baby nephew, who looked just like his father.

Since he was just an infant, Zaria remained the next heir to the throne. Soon, once he was old enough to start learning the politics of the kingdom, he would be crowned as the new heir.

She said that the baby was named Kalus after the Skyan word for strong mindset. His father had asked her to be his first guardian after his parents. She went on for the longest two pages of how excited she was to teach her nephew sword fighting. I smiled as I read the rant. If there was anything I had learned about her, it was that she could and would talk about something for hours.

"Something put you in a good mood." Adrian sets down a tray of cookies onto my desk.

"Yes, I've received a letter." I said as I popped a cookie into my mouth.

"From?" He asked me. I shrugged.

"A friend." That word felt a bit foreign on my tongue. I never had a true friend and it felt amazing to think I finally had one.

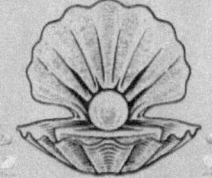

"You have friends?" Adrian said, and I was about to retaliate when I looked up from the letter at his face. He had a small smile plastered on his face and an emotion in his eyes that I hadn't seen in almost two years, pride. I had seen it in my mother's eyes many times, but it was different in his. It made something in my heart clench.

"I do..." I muttered. He nodded.

"Well, I have a letter for you too, but it's not from a friend. The royal ball is happening this year. Your attendance is mandatory." He handed me the invitation in the black envelope of the Magic Council's trademark.

"This again?" I groaned as I didn't even open the letter.

The royal ball was an event that was repeated every three years. I had been attending in place of my father since I was six. The Magic Council sent out an invitation to every royal family in Wyvern and invited them for a night of socializing. I understood it better as a way for them to show just how much control they had over the entire planet.

"I'll have suits prepared for both of us," Adrian said. I shook my head.

"No need. Just one for me and get Everett's measurements done." I said. Adrian looked at me with a face that said "are you serious" on it.

"It's about time he created connections." I started. He sighed and ran a hand through his red hair. Over the years, we had both grown a lot taller than we used to be. I could even reach high places without having to swim up to them. Adrian, although I had no evidence of it, had grown muscles. I wasn't even sure when he had time to work out between the art lessons with Everett and following my every move.

"He's 12."

"I won't let them bully him." I rolled my eyes.

"I'm supposed to be by your side at all times."

"It's one night. Nothing is going to happen."

"Fine, but I better not be hearing any sort of rumors after this."

"I promise." That was a lie. Little did I know that rumors were all that would surround me for the rest of my life.

56

"Zaria!" Everett nearly pounced on the girl. She failed to dodge in time, and they both fell backwards onto the ground. Mokoto, who was standing behind his sister, went down with them. The three of them lay on the ground on top of each other, groaning in the pain of the fall. Then, as if they were insane, they broke into an unsightly laugh. I wanted to bury myself in a cave and not come out for the next three hundred years. I could totally understand why Dragon Sukinaomo stayed as far away from others as possible. The entire room of royals all turned their eyes to the three kids on the floor.

"Please get up." I pleaded with them in a hushed whisper. After a second, they finally got up off the floor, and I fixed Everett's messy clothing.

"What do you do at this thing?" Zaria asked as she looked at the room full of people just standing around, talking to each other, and staring at us.

"Make connections," I said.

"That's it?" She made a disgusted face.

"Yes." I nodded my head. She made an exasperated sound and pouted.

"Is that a dessert table?" Mokoto spoke up from the silence, completely ignoring his twin's distress.

"Yep!" Everett smiled.

"Can I have some?" He asked.

"I think so! No one else is eating them." Everett explained, and before he even finished speaking, Mokoto was almost halfway to the table. Conveniently, right next to it stood a few royals I was required by my father to be on good terms with. I excused myself from saying hi to them.

When I finished my greetings, I went back to the spot where I had left my brother and Zaria to find them still there. The only difference was three new people standing next to them. They seemed to be talking as I approached.

"Yes, I'm an only child, so I can't sympathize. The tallest of the three spoke. He looked to be older than me, with brown hair, and what looked like leaves growing out of it. A nature folk. The land of nature had been split into more and more smaller kingdoms as the years went by, so I couldn't pinpoint exactly which kingdom he was a royal of.

"Oh, that sounds great! I have two younger brothers. They're so annoying." Another brown-haired boy, looking at Everett's age, spoke.

"I don't think my little sister is annoying, though. I love her." Zaria smiled.

"I only have an older brother, and he's very annoying." A girl with red hair, slightly deeper than Adrian's, and Zaria's height spoke. Her arms were crossed at her chest like she had a hundred better places to be than here.

"Me too, but mine is amazing!" Everett squealed. Then he spotted me and ran up to me. The entire group of kids turned to look at me. "This is him!" Everett did the poorest job introducing me. I only recognized the tall brown-haired boy, Justine Elios. King of Sheiza, the biggest and original kingdom of nature. He had the kindest brown eyes and a bigger build thanks to the fact that he was a bear. He was also five years older than me, making him an adult. He was originally crowned at the age of 16, five years ago, after his father was killed in war.

"Prince Bourne." He bowed his head, and I returned the gesture.

"King Justine."

"You know him?" Everett looked at me with a confused face.

"Yes, I've met the prince before at the last royal ball," I explained.

"This is Princess Lena of Boweth." Justine introduced me to the red-haired girl with grey eyes. She looked exactly like what I imagined Adrian would look like, a girl. But Lena's eyes were sharper, like everything around her was the most disgusting thing ever. They were cold and held a bit of black in them.

"Nice to meet you, princess." I bowed to her. She did a smaller bow to me, and her face scrunched up in disgust. I thought she was aiming to look at me before she spoke.

"Don't call me princess." The word princess was like a blade digging into skin when coming from her mouth.

"Then what would you like me to call you?" I asked, a bit intimidated by her presence. I don't think I need Justine to tell me what kingdom she hailed from, it was clear as day. Her posture was stiff, arms battered with scars, her hair tied up in her perfect ponytail, the aura of this girl who was no older than me exuded only one thing: the strength of the shadows. A pure daughter of war, as many Bowethian women were.

Boweth was the kingdom of shadows, a kingdom of war. Ruled by wolves, bloodthirsty creatures, the kingdom flourished under the absolute rule of its king. Every person born to that kingdom was taught how to fight both with and without a weapon in their hands. No one dared to upset the shadows..

"General." She spoke with a certain pride in it.

"Huh?" I let out louder than I meant to. Her eyes zeroed in on me, and I felt a chill run through my body. How did she have the exact presence of her father?

"I just mean, Bowethian generals aren't titled until they're twenty at least." I corrected myself, but it did nothing to extinguish the rage in her eyes.

"I know, I will be titled as soon as I turn twenty." She raised her chin up high with absolute confidence.

"How do you know that?" Zaria's voice came from behind her, and I saw the moment Lena's head whipped back to look at her. There was a tension I hadn't ever felt between the two girls as they made eye contact. A faceoff between a wolf and a hawk. Zaria's wings spread out slightly to take up more space and look more intimidating against the more muscled teenage girl. I wasn't sure if I should step in, but Justine, without hesitation, stepped in between them.

"My brother said that I will be," Lena growled.

"So, you'll let your privilege land you the role over your own abilities?" Zaria stated. I wasn't sure if she had a death wish or if she was just stupid. The two of them glared daggers at each other for a moment. Mokoto pulled his sister back with her arm with an annoyed look on his face.

59

"Well, I'm Prince Shinsui of Ita!" The brown-haired kid popped in with no situational awareness.

"Nice to meet you, Shinsui." Everett smiled. Mokoto and Justine took this distraction to pull the two girls apart and force them to face away from each other.

The rest of the ball was just us making sure that a fight didn't break out when we weren't looking. When we got back to our castle, Adrian was waiting for us. Everett ran up to him and started frantically explaining the entire night. Adrian just listened as he spoke with a small smile on his face. He looked up at some point, and our eyes met.

It's not like we hadn't made eye contact before, but this time it felt different for some reason. Like a spark went through my body for some reason. I'm not sure if he felt it too, but he looked back at my brother instead.

Chapter Eleven

Zaria had a best friend before Everett, his name was Christian Sylvester, and he was married to her oldest sister. Imagine my surprise at that. But there was more, Zaria knew every single knight personally, and they were all her friends. Ever since her parents had died the knights and servants of the castle had been raising her. You could tell just from how gentle and open they were that they all loved her so much. How does a crown princess have no noble friends but is close to her workers instead?

I had met Christian once and he felt like a big brother even to me. His face always had a smile, and he always held his baby in his hands as if he let the child go a minute without him, he would die. I was envious, my father never did that for me. He also felt fatherly towards the twins, offering small encouragement, head pats, and he never seemed to fall for their deception. He was also Skye's current head knight, so I could imagine how busy he was. Zaria told me that Christian is the one who taught her sword fighting, their father had entrusted the task to him. There was also Therian Kiser, Aquila's first cousin. He was the same age as the twins, so the three of them were close, but for some reason, they didn't talk anymore. That was a hard thing to do considering that, since he was the son of a noble family, he spent a lot of time in the castle. Every time I met someone new who was in any way related to the Aquila, I felt that this entire family was just a big anomaly.

Queen Suri Aquila was dead. Died in a war protecting her kingdom. Her son, barely a year old, was said to have died in a raid on the castle. Logically, this meant that Zaria would become queen, but she was only eleven years old. After careful deliberation by the Skyan nobles, it was determined that the second child, Akemi, would be the next queen. The only problem: she had no idea what she was doing. Zaria stepped up to help with most things. The action was very uncharacteristic of a child her age, but knowing Zaria, it somehow made sense.

There was no funeral for the dead queen and prince. Zaria said in her most recent letter to us that they were still rebuilding the kingdom, and the funeral would be done as soon as everything settled. I had reread the letter twice, but I could not find the heartache in her words. It was like she had removed herself from the situation, which was definitely not normal for a child. It broke my own heart. I wrote back immediately to let her know that I would help with anything if she asked. Her response was polite and a gentle way to say that she would handle it herself.

We could not make a visit because our father got sick around that time. As the princes of the kingdom, we were to help run the kingdom in his absence. I prayed for her at the temple of the goddess every day.

When our father recovered, the first thing Everett and I did was go to meet her. She greeted us at the castle gates with a smile on her face. She was dressed in a white dress, her hair tied back in braids that looked like a crown, her own crown sitting perfectly on top. Everett ran up and gave her a hug. Mokoto was by her side as always. Zaria's eyes looked tired and worn.

"Princess Zaria, my condolences." Adrian, who had decided to join us on this trip, spoke. Zaria smiled at him with a sad smile.

"Thank you." She said, "Come, let's get you some tea!" She turned and walked inside. As we followed her, many of the castle workers greeted us and smiled at Zaria, who greeted every one of them by name. The knights were scattered throughout the castle, just chatting with each other. The mood felt somber and less likely than it usually was.

"It's been like this since Chris was put on leave," Mokoto spoke and explained to us. Zaria didn't turn to look at us as she kept walking.

"Chris?" Everett asked.

"Our brother-in-law. He was the head knight." Mokoto said.

"Why is he on leave?" I asked, and Mokoto motioned his head towards his sister.

"I put him on leave," Zaria spoke. "He couldn't think properly, so I told him not to return until he was feeling better." Mokoto looked down at the ground now. We walked the rest of the way in silence.

She led us to the family parlor, filled with couches, glass shelves, and a giant piano in the center.

"Make yourselves comfortable. Maribeth, can you prepare the tea?" She asked the one maid who was going around dusting.

"Of course, your highness!" Maribeth rushed off to do as she was asked.

A few days later, the five of us were in the library. Adrian was exploring the aisles of books, Everett and Mokoto reading something at a table, Zaria had documents in front of her and a book off to the side. I was reading a newspaper I had found lying around.

"I think they're trying to kill me," Zaria spoke out of nowhere. We all looked up at her.

"What?" I asked, taken off guard by the statement.

"The nobles. They're planning something." She stated it so matter-of-factly that I questioned if she knew what she was even saying.

"Why do you think that?" Everett put down his book and looked at her, leaning forward like they were sharing a secret.

"Whispers, secret meetings, weird gifts. It's a feeling." She said, "But I can't put my finger on what it is."

"What are you planning to do?" I asked, also leaning forward. This sort of conversation usually happened in the safety of an office, not in the biggest library to exist, where anyone could be eavesdropping.

"I need evidence." She nodded her head to herself like this conversation was happening in her head.

"Maybe you're being paranoid?" I raised an eyebrow. Her's furrowed as she thought about it. Then she leaned back.

"Maybe..." She muttered. The conversation ended there as she slipped into her brain, having a conversation with herself. I looked over at Mokoto, who I recently found out could hear her thoughts. His eyebrows were also furrowed, and a worried expression rested on his face. He was biting his lips, trying to leave the conversation where it ended.

At the time, I really did think she was paranoid from spending so much time at court, but her suspicions only seemed to increase with every letter she wrote to us.

Chapter Twelve

Adrian and I were taking a stroll in the Skyan cloud gardens. I had reached for a blooming rose when the thorns dug into my fingers. I pulled back and watched as the red blood seeped out of my fingers. My water magic came with a healing element, so I wasn't too worried about this kind of injury, but Adrian seemed to be worried enough for both of us. He immediately started gushing over the blood, pulling a handkerchief out of his pocket and wrapping my hand with it. I smiled and lifted my head slightly to look at his face. That was when I noticed just how close we were. I could feel the brush of his breath even with the eternal Skyan wind around us. His grey eyes were looking straight into my purple ones, and I think my heart stopped.

"Thank you..." I muttered, and he nodded his head as he pulled away. For some reason, that disappointed me.

"You need to take better care of yourself." He whispered. I nodded in understanding. He started walking deeper into the garden, but I was stuck in my spot. I watched his back disappear.

"You're in love." I heard a voice say from behind me, and when I turned around, I was face to face with Zaria. I jumped back in fright. She had a stupid grin on her face.

"What?" I asked after I got hold of myself.

"With him. You're in love." She enunciated the word.

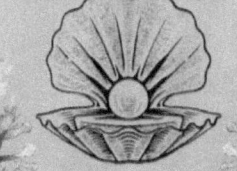

"No, I'm not." I shook my head. Me in love with Adrian? Never. He was so mean, and rude, and....

"It's slow, but it's happening." Zaria nodded. Her hands were behind her back.

"Wha-"

"I see these kinds of things..." Her smile turned sad for a second before defaulting back to the mischievous one. "It's best not to hide it... It just hurts you." She said, and then in a gust of wind, she was off into the sky. The weirdest girl I had ever known. Still, her words seemed to have left a mark on my brain. I started noticing things. Things I never paid attention to before.

A simple brush of our fingers, watching him tie his bangs out of his face when he painted, the small smirk he would have on his face when he succeeded in making me mad or annoyed. All of it was starting to be less annoying and more... captivating. It was getting harder to ignore him every day that passed.

More often, our eyes would meet and stay there longer than normal. But neither of us acknowledged this change in the atmosphere. It was unspoken, but there were hints.

He started walking in time with my steps, and instead of staying three paces behind me, he was right next to me. He would stay with Everett, teaching him until I came by to release him. I didn't need to, but he still waited, so I came every day. He'd lean over my shoulder when pointing out stuff in official documents instead of standing in front of the desk and pointing at it over the desk. There were small changes, but I still noticed every single one of them. At first, I thought they were in my head, but after it happened every day, you couldn't really say that.

"Are you dating Adrian?" Everett asked me one night as I helped him clean up his newest mechanical creation. Over the years, Everett has gone from taking apart stuff to building it.

"What?" I dropped one of the parts, and he reached out to catch it.

"Adrian. You're aid." He clarified, like I knew any other Adrian.

"No, no, I'm not dating my aide." I shook my head.

"You can tell me you know. I won't tell Father." Everett shoved the rest of his stuff into a box. I looked around his room, which had been filled with many paintings, some by him and some by Adrian.

"I'm not lying to you, Ev." I patted his head.

"I think you two would be good together." He whispered, but in the empty room it was very clear to my ears.

"Thank you for caring for my love life, Ev." I laughed. He smiled at me.

"I like him. He's nice and very fun to talk to." Everett admitted.

"Then I'm glad he's your art teacher." I smiled.

"I think he likes you." Everett looked into my eyes.

"Wait, what?" I blinked as my mind processed the new information.

"He's always talking about you..."

"In... a good way?" I pressed slightly.

"Yeah." Everett nodded. I wasn't sure exactly how to feel about that, but it did something to me knowing he talked about me to my little brother.

"He's single." I nearly choked.

"How do you know that?" I asked him.

"He was talking about it to a maid earlier today."

"Well, that's good for him." I coughed.

"No, he's single. That's sad." Everett shook his head.

"Maybe he wants to be single." I shrug.

"No, he was definitely complaining about it."

"Oh..." I really did not know what to say.

"It's like the books you read to me as a kid. You find love in unexpected places."

"Love?"

"He's nice but not too nice, and he helps you with work, he's charming, and handsome. He's a fairytale prince. Like in the books." I thought about it, really thought about it, and he was right. Adrian was probably the closest thing to a fairytale prince I would ever find, and he wasn't even a prince.

"Um, Ev... I, I have to go..." I muttered as I got up off the floor.

"He's in his room," Everett told me. I nodded as I swam out the door.

Just like he said, Adrian was in his room. I knocked on his door before I could regret my decision. He opened the door after a few seconds and looked at me with a raised eyebrow.

"Late night swim?" He asked. I nodded my head. I bit my lip as I came up with something to say.

"Actually, I didn't come for a swim..." I admitted.

"Then why are you here, Bourne?" My name on his tongue was different, and I think I liked it differently.

"I have something to say to you."

"I'm listening." He opened the door wider and crossed his arms to his chest.

"Um..." The confidence I had a few minutes ago vanished.

"Let me say something first." He held out a hand in front of me, stopping me from talking. I nodded my head, giving him space to speak.

"I want a raise." He spoke. That caught me off guard.

"What?" I blinked.

"Let's see, I'm your aid, go on business trips with you, and teach your brother." He listed it on his fingers. "And you just show up in front of my door whenever you want, so I want a raise."

"Oh, I can see what I can do..." I nodded.

"What did you want to talk about?" He asked, leaning against his door frame, looking all hot like men do in the books.

"You know it's not really important... good night..." I turned and started swimming away.

"Bourne Alion." He called after me. I stopped and turned around.

"Yes-" Before I could even think about it, his lips were on mine. I didn't know how to react for a second before he pulled away.

"You're supposed to kiss me back." He smirked, and I kissed him back. Over and over. Adrian's room, his bed, and his lips soon became my favorite places in the castle.

Chapter Thirteen

Father gotten sick again. The medic told me he didn't have much time left. No one knows this, but I think I broke out into a smile at the news. I knew that it was not appropriate, but I couldn't stop it. It was two months before my birthday that he called me into his bedchambers to talk.

He was in bed looking almost as pale as my mother had been when she was bedridden, but for him, I had no tears.

"Father." I greeted him, and his hand waved me over. I walked up to the side of the bed.

"Bourne." He spoke in a raspy voice. "Do not," a cough left his mouth, "ruin this kingdom." He finally finished. Then he shooed me away. I didn't expect anything else from him.

Only a few days later, he died in bed. I was crowned the next morning at the age of seventeen. It wasn't the youngest age for a crowning, so I didn't get a ton of backlash. The Alion family has been the ruling family for so long that it wasn't any surprise for me to be king either. It was actually a very quiet event.

What wasn't quiet was the first thing I did after becoming a prince.

I was on the training ground shooting some arrows when I felt Adrian behind me watching. Over the years, I had lost the need for a physical bow, having found a way to make one out of

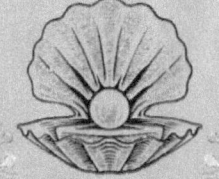

my water magic. I shot three arrows in a row, all landing exactly at their targets.

"Impressive, but you got some time for me?" Adrian asked. I disassembled my bow and walked back to him with a smile.

"Always." I kissed his lips. He smiled into the kiss and wrapped his hands around me. We pulled apart, and I wrapped my fingers around him. We swam to the coral gardens.

"So, what's it like being king?" He asked me, even though he already knew.

"So much more work." I laughed. "But I think handling the nobles is getting easier by the day." I smiled.

"That's good. I've been busy with paperwork as well." He shook his head. As I took over as king, the paperwork increased, and I handed the stuff I was working on before my crowning to Adrian. This helped me prioritize without losing time or progress on previous projects.

Adrian walked slightly in front of me and let go of my hand as he examined some of the coral. He was telling me something about them, but I really wasn't paying attention. I pulled out the box I had tucked in my pocket. Getting down on my knees, I opened the box and held it out in front of him before he finally noticed and gasped.

"What?" This is exactly how I planned it. Just like the books my brother reads.

"Adrian Castro... will you marry me?" I held the box in front of him with the coral ring I had spent two hours deciding on.

"Are you serious?!" He gasped again as he looked at the ring. "Oh, my goddess! Bourne! Yes!" He exclaimed, and I tackled him in a hug. We twirled in the water as uncontrolled laughter started from one of us, but quickly spread. I pulled him into our longest kiss yet.

Word spread as quickly as you would expect it to. People started talking; it wasn't like I had proposed in a quiet place. The coral gardens were always filled with staff, so someone must have heard and told someone else. It was fine with me. I was engaged to a man whom I loved.

When Everett found out he was jumping with joy, apparently, it wasn't just me who was beyond excited. He made me promise to ask him for his opinion on the decorations. So, when it came time to choose what color the banners were going to be, I made my way to his room.

"Ev!" I smiled as I entered. The room was empty, and everything was thrown around. I swam inside with worry. On the balcony, Everett sat on his sun chair with his tail pulled up to his chest. His head was buried in his scales.

"Ev?" I called out softly not to startle him. He slowly pulled his head up, and I could see how puffy and red his eyes were.

"Oh, Everett, what happened?" I swam up to him and sat at the side of the sun chair. He moved into my arms and I held him close to my chest, rubbing his back soothingly.

"Am I weird? He asked me, his voice cracking.

"No, you're not weird, Everett." I patted his back.

"The other kids can't do math like me... they said I'm weird and that making things is weird."

"That's not true... You have a gift." I pulled him back to look into his eyes.

"But a gift doesn't help me make friends." He cried. In my eighteen years of life, I had never really wanted friends as badly as I knew my brother did. At some point, that must have fled my mind. He probably felt so isolated here in the castle with only me and Adrian as his friends. His only other friends were Zaria and Mokoto, who lived too far to visit often. I didn't know what to say to him at that moment.

"They don't need to be your friends..." I spoke.

"I want them to be!" He shouted. The first time he had ever done that to me.

"Ev..."

"You don't get it! Everyone wants to be your friend!" He yelled.

"Stop yelling, Ev..."

"Get out!" he yelled. I felt a hot wave of rage rise in me. He had never yelled at me like that before.

71

"Fine!" I stood up and swam out of his room, closing it loudly behind me. After that, we didn't talk for weeks. It felt like torture, and when I tried to apologize to him, he avoided me. I had never had a serious fight with my brother before, so I had no idea what to do. Without a clue, I went to the only other person I could think of asking.

"Adrian, can I talk to you-" I stopped in my tracks as I opened the door to my old study, which he was using as his current office. Adrian was in the center of the room, his back to me, standing in front of the bookshelf, and I could see the figure of a person in front of him. His head whipped around to me, and he looked like he had been caught doing something wrong... He stepped back from the person and turned to me.

"Bourne!" He looked at me with wide eyes. The person, a girl, stared straight at me with a scared look.

"W-what is this?" My heart stopped at that second. My eyes started burning as I tried to explain it to myself in my head.

"It's not what you think!" Adrian took a step towards me. I backed away.

"No," I said, more to myself. Then I saw the slight swelling of the girl's lips and the hickey on her neck. "No..."

"Bourne..." His voice resonated in my head, but I couldn't bring my eyes back to him. She was wearing a staff uniform, her hair messy. Adrian's outfit was messy as well. I shook my head.

"No." It was the only word my mind could find. He stepped closer, and I did the only thing my body wanted to. I turned and swam away as fast as I could. I didn't even know where I was swimming to, just anywhere far away from here.

Chapter Fourteen

I had locked myself in my room for weeks. I sent a butler to kick both Adrian, and the girl he was with, out of the castle. All my food was delivered to my room, and I didn't attend any court meeting.

"Bourne..." Everett's voice came from my door, followed by a few knocks. I didn't respond.

"Please... can you open the door?" He pleaded but I just pulled my covers over my head drowning out all sound and light. I was not in the mood to talk to anyone. I knew he was out there calling to me for a while before it finally died down. After that for a whole month there was nothing from my door other than my food being delivered. I had closed the curtains cause the sunlight just seemed too cheerful for my depression.

A set of knocks came from my door. I ignored them just like I had for every other knock in the last two months.

"Bourne." A new voice came from my door. Zaria. Why was she here?

"Bourne, open the door. I'm not asking twice." She said, I pulled the covers over my head again. She wasn't actually here so I could just go back to sleep.

"Don't make me tear this door down." When I didn't respond the crazy girl actually *did* break the door down. I heard it open with a bang. I peeked my head out of the covers and in the rubble of floating wood, stood Zaria in a blue dress and a water helmet.

"Get out of that damn bed." She marched her way over to me and ripped my sheets straight off my bed. I couldn't even react fast enough to stop or stall her. Then she grabbed my hand and started pulling me out of bed. From the doorway, I saw Everett standing outside, staring in with wide eyes. Mokoto stood next to him, arms folded at his chest.

"Zaria! My door!" I gasped as it finally registered in my head that one Zaria Aquila was in Arco, and two, she had *broken* down my door like it was a piece of paper.

"I'll pay you back." She spoke.

"With what money?" I questioned.

"I never said when." She shook her head. At some point, she managed to get me off the bed and drag me out of the room. Everett and Mokoto followed behind us. She dragged me all the way to the dining room where the chef was standing, looking just as bewildered as I felt.

"Sit." She commanded me and forced me to sit in a chair at the table. Then she pushed me in and turned to the chef.

"Dinner. Now." She spoke in perfect Arcoian, and the chef rushed into the kitchen. She turned to her brother and my brother.

"Sit." She commanded them, too. They rushed into their own seats. She sat next to me. In a matter of minutes, the dinner was brought out and placed in front of us. Mokoto reached for his fork but stopped and put his hand down. All eyes landed on me. I instantly realized that they wanted me to eat first. I picked up my fork and started eating. I looked up at them, and they started eating as well. At some point, Zaria called a maid to fix my hair. According to her, it was disgusting.

A moment later, I looked at Zaria.

"Why are you here?" I asked her. She chewed and swallowed before setting her fork down.

"Your brother came crying to me. I had to knock some sense into you." She stated. I looked at Everett, who was avoiding eye contact.

"He swam all the way to the border, then walked the rest of the way," Mokoto said. My eyes widened as I finally took in Everett's disheveled appearance.

"Ev..." I called out. He looked up at me with red, puffy eyes.

"You wouldn't open the door...and I was worried... I didn't know who to go to..." He looked down again. I pushed my chair back and stood up. Next to me, Zaria stood up and took her brother by his arm, forcing him to drop his fork as she dragged him out of the room.

There was only me and Everett in the room. It was always just me and Everett. Since my mother died. Of course, he went to Skye. Zaria and Mokoto were the only friends he had besides me. I had locked myself away for two months, leaving him all by himself in this castle that was too big for just one person.

"Everett..." *Take care of your brother, please.* My mother's voice echoed in my head.

"I'm sorry." He apologized. I moved to the other side of the table.

"No. No. Don't be sorry, Ev. I'm sorry." I knelt next to his chair and took his hand.

"Bourne..." He called out in a broken voice. I broke down with him.

"I'm so sorry, Everett." I pulled him into a hug, and he clenched my shirt.

"I'm sorry too!" He cried onto my shirt. I closed my eyes and held him as close as I could. My little brother. I didn't need anyone else. Adrian didn't matter, not like Everett did. Adrian was just a boy. A boy I was dumb enough to give my heart and everything to. I was a king; I shouldn't have been that stupid. Look what it did to me; I abandoned my kingdom and only family.

That day, I made a promise to myself that I would always, always protect my little brother. He was my first priority in this life. I didn't need anyone else, especially not someone who would break my heart again. After all, I was born to be this kingdom's king and this little boy's big brother.

The End

The story continues in

The Eye of
the Storm

Support an Indie author
by leaving a review

Rosekwoodbooks.com
@rose.k.wood
@ros3_axtrism
Rosetheauthor12@gmail.com

ACKNOWLEDGMENTS

Oh! I'm back in less than six months! Writing this book was so much fun. I loved writing every second of it and inserting all the little secrets that I did. The next book has no set release date yet. I'm still writing it. Anyways, moving on to my acknowledgments.

I want to thank my best friend, Bread. She has been one of my biggest fans and supporters. I love her so much. She will always be the only person allowed to read my first drafts. The first real butterfly apart from me. When I told her I wanted to step back from writing book two for a while, she wholeheartedly supported me in starting this book. Bourne has always been one of my favorite characters ever. He is a lot like me in a scary way. I wanted to be genuine with him as I possibly could. Bread would read the small snippet I sent and fangirl over him with me. She was also the first pair of eyes helping me with editing. I love you so much bestie! Thank you so much!!

Now I want to thank my parents for everything. Although they never read my writing, I'm thankful for their support. Without them, Book One would've never been published. They are my rock.

I also want to thank my little brother for being the inspiration for Bourne and Everett's sibling dynamic. You'll always be my most important person. I love being your big sister, even if you annoy me all the time. He is the biggest help when it comes to putting some real-life logic in my writing and the fight scenes (even though there really was none in this book).

Finally, a big thank you to everyone who came from the first book! That includes my beta readers and everyone else. Thank you for reading my hard work. I strive to bring this world out of my head to all of you.

That's all for this book. Keep dreaming.

Welcome home, Butterflies.

Rose is a 19-year-old author who published her first book in July 2024. She is attending college and studying astronomy and writing. She has been writing stories for many years since she was a kid. She has published poems in her school journal. She is also doing editing on the side. She specializes in writing fantasy and found family trope. She has been experimenting with romance and other fantasy tropes.